THE LAST MUSTANG

Withdrawn fro

D0357632

Frank Bonham

The Last Mustang

Edited by Bill Pronzini

LEISURE BOOKS NEW YORK CITY

LEISURE BOOKS ®

October 2004

Published by

Dorchester Publishing Co., Inc.
200 Madison Avenue
New York, NY 10016

If you purchased this book without a cover you should be aware
that this book is stolen property. It was reported as "unsold and
destroyed" to the publisher and neither the author nor the publisher
has received any payment for this "stripped book."

Copyright © 2003 by Gloria Bonham and Bill Pronzini.
Additional copyright information on pages 207–208.

All rights reserved. No part of this book may be reproduced or
transmitted in any form or by any electronic or mechanical means,
including photocopying, recording or by any information storage
and retrieval system, without the written permission of the
publisher, except where permitted by law.

ISBN 0-8439-5432-9

The name "Leisure Books" and the stylized "L" with design are
trademarks of Dorchester Publishing Co., Inc.

Printed in the United States of America.

Visit us on the web at www.dorchesterpub.com.

Table of Contents

City of Devils   13

The Last Mustang   54

River Man   74

Payment Past Due   93

Good Loggers Are Dead Loggers   110

Burn Him Out!   138

The Bronc' Stomper   156

One Man's Gold   172

Foreword

by
Bill Pronzini

Before he turned exclusively to Western and young adult novels in the early 1950s, Frank Bonham contributed scores of short stories and novelettes to pre- and post-World War II magazines. Nearly all of these were either Western or historical in nature, and appeared in such top-line adventure pulps as *Blue Book*, *Argosy*, and *Short Stories* and in such action Western periodicals as *Dime Western*, *New Western*, Street & Smith's *Western Story*, and *Zane Grey's Western Magazine*.

As with the stories in two previous Bonham collections, THE CAÑON OF MAVERICK BRANDS (Five Star Westerns, 1997) and STAGE TRAILS WEST (Five Star Western, 2001), the selections here give ample evidence of his abundant storytelling abilities. These strengths include extensive research and attention to historical detail, colorful backgrounds, a wide variety of well-developed characters, innovative handling of familiar themes, and rousing action sequences.

Early Los Angeles and the fading grandeur of the Spanish *rancheros* is the locale of "City of Devils", a swift-paced account of manipulation and treachery among greedy cattle interests seeking to supply much-needed meat to the miners of northern California. Sam Ware, a hard-bitten young opportunist, learns a harsh lesson about honesty, loyalty, and trust when he joins forces with an unscrupulous megalomaniac, General George Tate, in a scheme to fleece a struggling Mexican *don*.

"The Last Mustang" is a good-humored saga of Wild-Horse Farnum, a mountain-bred mustanger whose heart is as big as his loneliness and who plays "the part of a one-man Wild West show, but always he would peer at himself doubtfully from various angles in an attempt to see how he looked to other people." A job trapping a herd of wild horses in the Whetstone Mountains leads to something much more than he bargained for—a case of cattle rustling and a woman rancher who poses a severe threat to his fiddle-footed freedom.

"River Man" demonstrates Bonham's lifelong fascination with various modes of transportation in the Old West. In this tale, the mode of travel is a Missouri River steamboat during the Civil War. The protagonist, Davey Leathers, is a young cub pilot whose education in the ways of the Big Muddy include the river lore of a salty old veteran pilot and a furious battle with a band of Confederate guerrillas.

Redemption for past sins and lost opportunities is the theme of "Payment Past Due". An aborted stage hold-up acts as catalyst to give Sam Sullivan, an Easterner haunted by personal demons, a new lease on life as the first doctor in the Arizona pueblo that would one day become Tucson.

Fast and furious action is the hallmark of "Good Loggers Are Dead Loggers", which pits an Oregon cattleman against careless timber men cutting trees to make railroad ties. Jim Crockett, joined by feisty old printer and newspaperman Ed Harney, not only battles the logging interests but the Sacramento & Mountain City Railroad Company as well through a succession of fistfights, logjams, dynamited tracks and derailment, and a final showdown by fire.

"Burn Him Out!" is Bonham at his most suspenseful. The subject matter here is a literal plague of grasshoppers, and the desperate efforts of a group of ranchers led by Will Starrett to halt the insects' devastating advance across their grasslands.

"The Bronc' Stomper" is Cal Hawkins, a cowboy reluctant to give up his rodeo career despite advancing age, a net balance of four hundred dollars at the end of his last season, and seven well-knit fractures. His encounters with a high-spirited horse named Iron Duke and the equally high-spirited Joyce Taverner bring him to a crossroads in his life, and give him a better understanding of "that intangible thing called pride."

Another stirring action tale, "One Man's Gold", features Casey Brent, a faro dealer hired by promoter Bob Harvey whose business is buying up defunct ranches and played-out mines. Casey's job is to protect Harvey's interest in a failed ranch from the niece of the deceased owner and from a pair of gold-hunting squatters. Casey soon discovers, however, that neither Harvey nor the niece or her dead uncle's apparent suicide or the ranch property itself are quite what they seem to be. In an explosive climax he also discovers that every man, including himself, prizes a different form of gold.

Bill Pronzini
Petaluma, California

City of Devils

I

"THE MAN FROM TEXAS"

The big man with the windy voice had penned his cattle on a bench across the creek from town. Sam Ware had run down with every other able-bodied man to watch the bidding on the steers. The mining country was starved for meat—good, stringy beef that gave your teeth a fight, anything to break the monotony of spuds, beans, and dried apples. Drought had burned the cattle country to the south until the steers they drove north from Los Angeles collapsed before they had even made Sacramento.

Sam Ware, who had an eye for a quick dollar, thought: *I'd like to be in that Texan's boots.* He had fifty steers—at least they had horns and legs hanging down at the corners—and the prices he would get for those Texas steers should make him a comparatively rich man.

The big drover raised both hands as he sat in the saddle before the stone corral. Three cowpunchers sat their ponies within the enclosure.

"Little quieter, boys!" the man shouted. "Don't scare the cattle. Now, then, I hear you bidding against each other. Gentlemen, get this straight . . . I'm not figuring to auction a single head of stock."

A wide-shouldered, heavy-jowled man, he sat a deep saddle with the skirts of his coat hanging back to expose bone handles of a pair of Colts. His thighs were thick, his face was wide and dark, and his hair was iron gray, streaked white down the middle like the head of a badger. There were theatrics in his bearing, as if he had come all the way across the plains just for the relish of this moment.

"No, sir," he continued, "I ain't going to auction them. That wouldn't be fair to you. You're beef hungry. You're excited. You might pay three dollars a pound for these critters, and after you got a belly full of beef and the fit passed, you'd claim old Tate hadn't given you a square shake. By the way," he added, "I'm George Tate. They call me General Tate down in Deaf Smith County. Any you men from Deaf Smith County? Like to shake your hands if you are."

It appeared there weren't any other Deaf Smith expatriates.

Tate went on: "So it's going to be outright sale. A dollar and a half a pound. There was a time when I figgered ten dollars wasn't enough, when the Seminoles were raiding us in Kansas. You'll notice some figgers painted on the sides of these animals. That was done by a public weigh master. So that's the way it's going to be, fellers, and you can just point out your critter, and the boys will cut him out for you. First man!"

He leveled his arm at a big, bearded man in a butcher's apron near the front of the crowd. The sale started. It gave Sam Ware goose-flesh to see the way the gold pieces chinked into Tate's saddlebag.

A notch-eared shorthorn cross, various brands, nine hundred and seventy pounds brought $1,455.00. "Knock off the fifty-five because of all them brands," Tate ordered. "He's probably already half cooked!"

They laughed, and continued to dump their easy gold into his *aparejo*. Butchers got first choice, and most of them

14

took several animals. The buyers for out-of-town mines shouted their choices, and finally little gangs of men who would butcher their own beef and split it.

All this time General George Tate kept up an endless patter. But when the last steer had been turned over to its owner and the crowd started to leave, his manner changed like—Sam thought—an actor's might as he stepped from the stage to say: "I'd like to get my hands on that damned fool in the third row with the paper bag."

He paid off his men. Sam noted that they split up without shaking hands. Then Tate stood, rubbing his palms slowly together and watching the crowd drift back across the bridge and up the hill. As he did so, he noticed Sam Ware. He didn't look pleased to see Sam start toward him, but he sat his saddle waiting.

Sam was a large, dark-haired young fellow with a taste for relaxations that did not necessarily have to involve young women but preferably did, women who spoiled him a little, and this showed in an over-casual walk that seemed to involve his shoulders as much as his feet, and in a trace of vanity about his mouth. He wore a buckskin shirt and well-tailored trousers, carrying at his left hip an ivory-handled Dragoon Colt worn butt foremost, cross-draw fashion. He had found it difficult to learn to draw the gun that way, but it was the unusualness of it that appealed to him.

He stopped by the corral and put up his hand. "Sam Ware, General."

Tate, after an instant's hesitation, reached down. Up close, grooves showed in the big, slightly dished face—lines that talked of ladies loved and bottles drained in the gray pre-dawn hours. He was a man of fifty with a curving mustache above a small mouth and stiff eyebrows darting up at the corners like the devil's own.

15

He said: "Pleased to meet you, Ware."

"Had quite a time with those Seminoles in Kansas, eh?" Sam remarked. "I was thinking they must have been right tuckered, after that trip. The last time I heard of the Seminoles, they were in Florida."

Tate's obsidian eyes had frost needles in them. "They might have been Kaws." He shrugged.

"Must 'a' been. You know, General," Ware said suddenly, "I've been knocking around Nevada City quite a spell, but I haven't run into any public weigh masters. Where'd you have those cattle weighed, if I'm not too curious?"

"Curious?" Tate drawled. "Nosy, I'd say. Why, I had them weighed in Sacramento, and if you want proof . . . not that it's any of your damned business. . . ."

He was reaching for a paper in his inside coat pocket, and Sam was a little uneasy to catch the flash of a shoulder gun, in addition to his other Colts. He said hastily: "It doesn't matter to me personally, but it would, if I'd bought any steers, because in that valley heat they'd have dropped twenty, twenty-five percent of prime weight walking up from Sacramento."

Tate placed both hands on the flat Mexican horn, and leaned over the swell. His manner had a slowed-down, guarded quality. "Young fella," he said, "you're making sounds like somebody that's looking for. . . ."

Sam suddenly grinned. "Easy, General. If those fellows were willing to pay your price, why, it's nothing to me. All I was wondering . . . well, it seems to me you would have got your money just as easy by raising the price a bit and admitting they'd lost weight. And then nobody'd have a comeback."

There was in his grin something that pierced the big

16

drover's anger. General George Tate winked. "Son, it's the difference between trapping a bear and stalking him. It's the element of chance. There's just a chance he might get you first. But it's a damned slim chance, and you can take a little pride in bragging about the hide later on." He winked again. "Time for a drink, Sam?"

"Time for almost anything," Sam told him.

In an oblique way, it was disclosed that Sam Ware was tired of mining and looking for something equally profitable but not so rigorous. There seemed to be a little thorn in the seat of Sam's pants that kept him from ever sitting in one place long. Similarly it came out cautiously, just the edge of the fact showing, that General Tate had such a project in mind. "A little deal in cattle, Sam. Down in Los Angeles. The City of Angels. I must 'a' visited it at the wrong season . . . never saw a thing but devils, male and female. I reckon on some profit out of this, though."

"But the drought's about cleaned the *ranchos* out, hasn't it?"

Tate nodded. "No feed, no money, thousands of cows. And the way it happens, I need a feller to go down there with me."

"What for?"

Tate sounded hurt. "The Mexes don't like me, Sam. I fought against them at San Gabriel, during the war. I need a . . . well, call it an agent."

Sam considered. "Don't get me wrong," he said in a moment. "I don't particularly like hard work, but at the same time I wouldn't like swinging from a rope or scooting out of town ahead of the Vigilantes. Just what did you have in mind?"

Tate winked. "Tell you that, boy, and I'd give away the

hottest thing in twenty years. It's take it or leave it. But I'll tell you about this deal you just witnessed, and you can judge from that. Those cattle came from Nevada. I found a rancher who didn't know there was a shortage over here. That's the truth. But I tacked on the Texas yarn to keep men from asking the same thing you did, because it looked suspicious that a man two hundred miles away wouldn't know about the California market."

For an instant longer, Sam was kept from speaking by some stern monitor in his brain. It was obvious that whatever Tate had in mind, it was somewhat irregular. It would mean hewing so close to the line that you brought half the line away on your axe. But it also would mean adventure. It was this consideration that finally caused him to put out his hand.

"All right, General. Will you make me a captain if I join your army?"

"Captain!" scoffed Tate. "Why, there's major's leaves on your shoulders right now!"

II

"CITY OF DEVILS"

This was the way Sam Ware and General George Tate discovered that their destiny was to come, for a time at least, wrapped in a single package. It was the start of a careless odyssey that took them down the Sacramento River on a steamboat, that led through some wild times on the Barbary Coast of San Francisco, and eventually saw them crossing the gangplank of a disreputable coasting schooner. The master was a man by the name of Morrissey. He was an erect, white-haired man with a tight smile that hid a set of cheap false teeth. But he did not smile often. His customary demeanor was a frowning silence. Yet sometimes Sam Ware suspected a prior acquaintanceship between him and the general, something he could only guess at because of an inflection or a glance.

On a warm day in mid-October they hove to off Dead Man's Island, in what Los Angeles called her harbor. Low brown hills came down to the water, and in a wide inlet there were briny sloughs where Mexicans had their huts. But there were no docks, no way to bring a boat in, and a longboat was put over the side.

Captain Morrissey stood by the davit as the deck hands were about to lower the boat. "A thought occurs to me," he said. "I'll make this port again in about two weeks. Might it be you'd have your business in hand and a cargo to ship?"

"It might be." Tate smiled. "Some hides, some tallow. What day would you say?"

"Hell, let's say the Twenty-Seventh. They tell me there is wild hay for the cutting farther down the coast, where the drought hasn't touched."

The seamen ran the longboat up on the beach, and Sam and the general jumped out. Some Mexicans came from the huts. Children and dogs ran yelping down the beach. Standing there with his carpetbag in his hand and his shoulders back, breathing the clear warm air, Sam liked the feel of the country. It fitted him like an old coat—tranquil, no drive, no restlessness, a country for sleeping.

They rented horses and started for the pueblo fifteen miles away. On the way they could see the effects of the drought in hills and mesas burnt brown, gaunt cattle browsing on sere fuzz. There were withered vineyards where they stopped and picked bunches of grapes, dry as raisins. In late afternoon they began to enter the town.

Scattered adobe houses gathered into semi-regular blocks. They passed many more vineyards, some orange groves watered by willow-fringed *zanjas*. The heart of the pueblo was only a few blocks square, consisting of brick buildings and a preponderance of whitewashed mud structures.

Open-air butcher shops attracted buzzing clouds of flies, while stables contributed their hot animal odors. Crows seemed to be everywhere, along the eaves of the buildings, congregating in the streets.

Tate, seeming to know where he was going, steered to the Bella Union Hotel, a tall, slot-like building on the plaza. They took a room, shaved, and emerged in the early night on a dark street spiced with foreign odors and humming with the sounds of distant music and voices, the *clopping* of horses, a woman's shrill voice berating her man on a street corner.

Tate began to walk, but Sam, under the prodding of an uneasiness, said soberly: "General, I'm thinking it's about time you took the blinders off. If there's easy money to be picked up honestly, I'm for it, but otherwise. . . ." He made a gesture with his cigarette.

The big man at his side laid a hand affectionately on his shoulder. "All right, son. Here it is. You saw those ranches we passed on the way up? Those Mex *rancheros* are about to fold up. Most of them are still Mexicans, though a few Yankees have got their wedges in. But there's going to be one more Yankee in business tomorrow. And, Sam. . . ." He hesitated, and in the soft glow from a mescal shop his face was a mixture of enthusiasm, greed, and the holy consecration of an acolyte. "Sam, he's going to be the biggest Yankee that ever hit this town! They call this the Queen of the Cow Counties, and she's going to have a king. General George Tate!"

Unmoved by his ardor, Sam asked coolly: "What am I going to be . . . the court fool?"

Tate laughed. "The prime minister. See if you can poke any holes in *this* plan. You buy in as pardner with some hard-up Mex. You're a fifty-one percent pardner, and what you say goes. No more *fiestas* while the cattle eat grapes in the vineyard. No more *bailes* while the oranges dry up for lack of irrigation and the cattle lose themselves. *That's* the trouble with this country, Sam . . . lack of common sense! A man with a little capital and ordinary sense could take over this country in ten years' time." He squinted. "I've got a friend. Name of Cowden, an attorney. He knows 'em all. He'll know which are ripe for picking. So, y'see, we're not going to hurt anybody but the loan sharks. We'll put somebody on a paying basis, and we'll do ourselves some good, too. I'm cutting you in for a third share just for fronting for me until things look right. Well," he asked, "will you have to clear that with your parson?"

Sam was relieved. He smiled. "When do we start, General?"

"We're already started. We're going to see Will Cowden tonight."

There was a small adobe office building between a blacksmith shop and a general store. A wooden sign projected over the street: **LIC. WM. COWDEN, ABOGADO, ATTY. AT LAW.** The windows were screened halfway up with green cloth and glowed gently with lamplight. Tate rapped. A man came from an inner room to meet them. He was short, stocky, dark with full sideburns, and large eyes that studied them carefully as they stood in the dusk of the street.

"Howdy, Will," Tate said.

Cowden visibly started. Then he said: "Well, George! Come in, come in!" He let them into his office, into the smell of dust and cowhide-covered books and a scent of cooking. He shook hands with both men, but Sam thought he had the flushed, rumpled air of a man interrupted at lovemaking.

"George, this . . . this is great!" he said. "Hadn't expected you back from Frisco so soon."

He had them sit on the oak-and-rawhide settee while he sat behind his desk. He set out liquor and cigars, but he never lost that air of discomfiture. There was good-natured talk, but not once did General Tate's eyes leave their perusal of Cowden's face. At last he said: "Sam, here, is helping me out. You can talk free. Let's get down to business, Will."

Cowden's heavy eyebrows went up a trifle. "You mean the . . . ?"

"You know what I mean," Tate rapped.

Sam saw the attorney's glance flick to a shelf of books fixed against the wall. He cleared his throat, and handled his cigar very carefully as he rubbed the ash into a saucer.

"George," he said, "things haven't worked out. I was thinking of Bonifacio Guerrero before, you know. He came into a little money somehow, so he's out. And there was Bandini in the cards, too, but he. . . ."

Tate got clumsily to his feet. "You're a damned liar! Things are tighter now than they've ever been. You know that. Will, if you try to deal to me off the hind end of the deck, I'll. . . ."

Cowden, alarm in his large, limpid eyes, fussed with the cigar and looked almost imploringly at Tate. "That's not

22

fair, George! I write practically every paper that's drawn up in this town, and I know what I'm saying."

Tate continued to stare at him. He said slowly: "Let's see . . . old Guerrero had a daughter, didn't he? You ain't thinking of marrying a ranch, are you?"

Color leaped into the lawyer's face, and the grin he managed seemed tailored for a much smaller mouth—it barely clung to his lips. It was the furtive face of guilt he showed, and from Tate it brought a sound like a bull's regurgitation.

"You scum!" he shouted. "You're lower than corral shovelings! You. . . ."

He was still shouting as he seized Cowden's black cloth tie and dragged him halfway across the desk. He began to club at his face with the edge of his knuckles. Cowden cried out and tried to tear loose. He continued to get the chopping angle of Tate's fist across the nose, the eyes, the mouth. He was bleeding and beginning to make sounds like sobs when Sam dragged Tate away.

"You'll kill him," he said.

Tate thrust him away, a look of dark fury on his flat face. "What do you think I'm trying to do?" He reached for the lawyer again, but, when he saw that Cowden had slipped away from the desk and lay on the floor, he stopped and made a settling motion with his shoulders into the black frock coat. He snatched his hat from the settee, and walked to the door.

More slowly, with a look of concern at Cowden, Sam followed him. They went out into the night. Suddenly Tate turned and drove his fist angrily against the adobe wall twice. "The dirty, stinking . . . ! The set-up of a lifetime, and a mincing tinhorn lawyer cuts me out of it!"

Sam somehow got him to a saloon. A monte game was

going on and a horde of Americans, Mexicans, and men of assorted nationalities crowded the table. A slim Mexican girl with a chocolate-colored cigarette in her lips slipped between them at the bar. *"¿Quiere Josefina?"*

Sam said no. The girl spat her smile at him in a curse, and departed. Sam looked about. They had not learned to enjoy their pleasures yet in this town. They took things too seriously. At the moment Tate was taking his drinking pretty seriously, too, and Sam started a campaign to taper him off and get him back to the hotel. Cowden's treachery had stripped his good nature from him utterly.

They reached the hotel around midnight. Tate was weaving a bit but still in his black mood. "I could put a bullet through his head," he said, "and they'd never find out who did it. You can get away with anything here. It's the dirtiest city in America, and he's the dirtiest pig in it."

Sam had been doing a little thinking. "General, did you say he managed the Guerrero place?"

Tate had pulled off his coat, and now stood by a barred window opening on a stable, removing his pleated white shirt. "Rancho San Rafael, twelve miles northwest of here."

"Did you see him look at that stack of account books on the shelf when you asked him about Guerrero?"

Tate turned. His hard, creased, brown face began to soften. "Sammy," he said, "I knew there was a reason why we met. You're good for me. You're my rabbit's foot. We'll bust in there, lug his books back here, and see whether Guerrero can look the tax collector in the eye."

He took the play out of Sam's hands, hastily dressing once more and slapping on his hat. They left the hotel. The streets were quiet now. They left Los Angeles Street and found themselves on a thoroughfare hardly wider than an alley, crowded on both sides with one-story adobes. Garbage and refuse littered the road, awaiting the arrival of crows in the morning. Suddenly Tate stopped.

"This is the back of his place. His yard's across that wall. One of us will have to go in from the front, though, or he'll hear us sure. The door will be locked, and it won't be any ten-cent padlock. It'll take a shoulder against the door to break it."

He was opening a reeling gate in the mud wall. Sam had a glimpse of a yard jumbled with trash, of a geranium vine ascending wildly from a tangle of weeds to the roof. A barrel of papers stood near the back door.

Tate grunted. "There we are. A match in that barrel, son, and it'll be a clear field for you."

Sam saw that he had been awarded the job of breaking into the office, but Tate was still heavy with liquor. "Give me five minutes," he said.

He walked briskly to the corner, walked left to the next, turned left again, and reached a point halfway down the block, a hundred feet from General Tate but with the solid block of stores and offices between them. Cowden's office was dark. On the walks there were no passers-by, only a dog limping along inspecting heaps of refuse.

Suddenly he heard a hoarse shout: "Fire!" He saw scarlet threads of flame soaring above the roof, and within the building the lawyer knocked something over and his boots struck the floor with a *thud*.

Sam tried the door. It gave a half inch. He drew back a foot and lunged against it. The door held. Once more he hurled his weight against the heavy panels, and again he felt the shock to his heel. This time a screw screeched in dry wood. Growing alarmed, Sam hit the door with all his force, knowing he could not make much more noise without being heard.

He went through and fell to his knees on a mat on the dirt floor. He scrambled up, and stood an instant, listening. He heard the back door *bang*. He reckoned Cowden had come back for a bucket of water and run out again.

In three strides, he reached the bookshelf and held the first, fat volume to the faint, ruddy light coming from the rear. **Cuentas,** he read, **Bandini . . . de la Buerra . . . Lugo. Accounts.** He tried another book. **Vasquez . . . Gardea . . . Noriega.** The third ledger was the one. **Obregon . . . Guerrero.**

Sam turned hastily. As he did so, he saw the man who stood in the doorway with something in his hand that ran fluidly with the cold yellow of firelight on steel. He heaved the ledger across the room, saw a dazzling rush of burning gases from the muzzle of the revolver, and heard the bullet smash into the shelf at his back. Then he saw that Cowden had taken the heavy cowhide ledger in the brisket, and stumbled back.

He hurled another book, a third, a fourth, and sprang across the room toward the lawyer to take him before he could recover from the barrage. Cowden was on hands and knees.

Sam got a handful of undershirt and pulled him up. He slammed him fully in the face. Cowden collapsed. Sam had the thought that it had been a black day for Will Cowden when he and Tate came to town. Within a few hours, he had been whipped by both of them.

He groped around until he found the ledger, tucked it under his arm, and ran out the front. When he reached the walk, he started at a fast walk for the hotel.

III

"BULLETS FOR THE YANKEES"

In the morning they examined the account book. Bonifacio Guerrero appeared to be a long way from prosperous. He had outstanding debts totaling $7,800. Although this was the reason for selling beef, he had taken in little money. His grape and wine profits were small. There were other irregularities, as well. Cowden had been robbing him blind.

Tate brought the pages of the book together with a boom. "That's it, Sammy! Maybe you can even take this girl away from him. No split on that one, if you do." He laughed. But Sam saw that the disillusioned eyes in the rugged face were watchful.

"If I'm going to do it," he said, "I'll have to have the cash on deposit somewhere."

"On deposit! There's no bank in this hole. You carry it in your saddlebag." From under the bed Tate swung the rawhide sack in which he had brought the money. He opened it, and took out a sheaf of bills that he tucked quickly inside his coat. "That leaves forty thousand. That's why I'm putting the curse on this money in case you ever get any idea about swindling me out of a dime of it. Buy in with him as cheap as you can. There's a paper in the bag. Just fill in the amount. You and I will have a side agreement that you'll sell two-thirds of your share to me for a dollar, on demand. After they get used to having a Yank around, I'll walk in."

Sam shouldered the money. He hesitated a moment, then put out his hand. "See you soon, General."

"So long, Sam. Oh . . . !" Tate pulled a scrap of paper from his pocket and handed it to him. "Little map of where

I'll be camped. Drop around in about a week and let me know how it's going."

Sam rode from the pueblo. Following directions, he swung toward a gap in a high mole of gray-green hills. In the middle of the afternoon he entered Verdugo Cañon, a wide, tree-choked valley cutting through the hills to a higher valley beyond. In about two miles, he caught sight of a spread of whitewashed buildings screened by oak and pepper trees.

He crossed a bridge, and entered the yard. There was every sign of prosperity—many workers in view, well-kept corrals and barns, and a thick coat of whitewash on the long two-story building facing him. He knew these meant expense, not profit.

A small bowlegged man in tight *vaquero*'s pants and jacket approached him. Sam said: "I seek *Don* Bonifacio."

" *'Ueno,*" said the Mexican, smiling under his downsweeping black mustaches, a small and pompous man with hair carefully plastered down. "I am Montes, the *mayordomo*. It is my pleasure to carry you to *Don* Bonifacio."

Sam sat for a few minutes in a large, low-ceilinged parlor. There was a harpsichord, plain rawhide furniture, mats on the floor instead of rugs. The adobe walls were two feet thick. Blue glassware set in the sills caught the fire of the late sun. While he sat there working on his speech, a tall, old man entered with a girl at his side.

Sam shook hands with the man, but his attention was for the girl. She was Mexican, with the surprising coloring of the well-born Mexican woman, her complexion creamy and rich, her hair lustrous. Her eyes were the deep blue of hyacinths. She smiled as they shook hands, a cordial smile

28

that made guilt creep through Sam.

The old man was speaking. "A pleasure, *Don* Samuel. Will you make yourself comfortable, in this house which is yours?"

It was an effort to meet the old man's eyes. Everything they said threw it up to him that he was a spy here, an interloper. Guerrero was a very tall, white-haired, bearded old man with eyes full of sadness. Sam looked in them and saw the death of the old days, the time of *fiestas* and graceful indolence.

They talked endlessly, but at last he realized that craft, with such people as these, was beyond him. He decided to be blunt, almost hoping that Guerrero would be offended. "*Don* Bonifacio," he said, "I am a businessman. I enjoy talking with you, but I did not come here to talk. I came to offer you a way out of bankruptcy."

Guerrero appeared puzzled. "Am I to be declared bankrupt?"

"I . . . I don't know," Sam said. "I guess almost all you big ranchers are. You see, I . . . I've got some money to invest. I'm offering thirty thousand dollars for a fifty-one percent interest in your land and stock."

Guerrero looked at Tonía, the girl. He smiled and nodded. He said softly: "You see, the *padre* was right."

Tonía smiled again at Sam. "We prayed that we would not have to borrow. Once a *ranchero* borrows, he is through. *Don* Sam, you are sent of God."

Sam was shocked and ashamed. He was on his feet angrily. "Of God? How do you know the devil didn't send me? Why should I be honest when half the Yankees in Los Angeles are thieves?"

The old man peered at him. "You have an honest face," he said seriously.

Sam's fingers dug through his hair. "An honest face! It takes more than varnish to make a good piece of furniture, my friend."

"Then we ask you," Tonía said severely. "*Do* you intend to cheat us?"

Sam sat down, baffled. "No. But if you accept me as a partner, I'll change the place so you'll never know it. No more *bailes* . . . no more whitewashing barns when the cattle are starving for grain."

"It is what San Rafael needs," Guerrero agreed gravely. "You have money in the city?"

"I've got it all with me. And the paper for you to sign."

Sam brought the saddlebag inside. He watched Guerrero put his trembling signature onto the paper. He watched him put the money in a cracked wooden safe, without counting it. Then the old man struck his hands together.

"*¡Eso!* After good fortune . . . *la fiesta!* We will send out word to all the pastures that one week from today the fattest beeves will be barbecued, the best wine. . . ."

Sam shook his head. "Tomorrow we will start a range count. Those beeves will go to market after the rains start. The wine will go to San Pedro to wait for a boat. After our first year in the black, we'll think about a *fiesta*."

Sam was given a bedroom off the patio. Through the carved wooden bars he saw a dry fountain, languid rose vines, trees loaded with fruit. He fell asleep thinking of how Tonía had looked when she said: *Don Sam, you are sent of God.*

In the morning Guerrero assembled a small army of *vaqueros*. Montes, the mustachioed *mayordomo*, spurred officiously about. Vicente, the corporal, sat solemnly in a wooden saddle with a bundle of sticks under his arm. A dozen *vaqueros*, grinning self-consciously every time Sam looked at one of them, waited for what would happen.

Sam had studied a plan of the ranch. There were a hundred and eight square miles of valley and mountain land to be covered. He planned to hit the Noche Buena pasture, in the upper valley, first. During this operation the ranch could serve as range headquarters. As they prepared to ride out, he stopped beside the range foreman, Vicente.

"What are the sticks for?"

Vicente's long face wrinkled. "They are for the tally. One notch for ten cows. Fifty notches to one stick. One stick, five hundred cows."

Sam smiled, thinking of the difference one lost stick might make in feed calculations.

That day they worked the foothills, currying the dry brush jungles for outlaw cattle. Sam left Montes in charge of the tally. With Guerrero, he inspected the valley for springs. He found a few seeps where a week's work with a shovel would make a passable tank to hold water for the cattle. He made notes of these things, and the Mexican had nothing to say but: "*Sí, hombre.* It will be done."

They returned to San Rafael in the dusk to find Tonía standing at the bridge with Will Cowden, the attorney.

Across the bridge of Cowden's nose was a deep cut. His lips were swollen and one eye was half-closed. Tonía watched with arch suspicion as Sam dismounted. She said: "You were right. Not of God, but of the devil."

Guerrero, puzzled, glanced at Will Cowden. Cowden's voice was a restrained shout. "Didn't I tell you never to sign anything without consulting me? This partner of yours is one of a gang of cow thieves!"

Guerrero stared at Sam.

31

Sam said stiffly: "He's a liar."

"Liar!" Cowden yelled. "Do you deny that you came to my office with that scoundrel, Tate, and tried to force me to give information on my clients? That you broke into my office night before last and stole the ledger with the Guerrero account in it?"

Sam thrust his fingers under his belt and regarded the lawyer thoughtfully. "I deny that I'm a cow thief. Do you want me to tell the whole story?"

Cowden's battered face held a glint of triumph. He said: "Naturally. But you'll tell it in the pueblo. Lift your hands."

Sam started. Then he realized that it was not the lawyer's gun he had to fear, but another's—someone who even now had him under his sights. He glanced about and saw a man who leaned in the fork of a tree about fifty feet away, the stock of a rifle against his cheek.

He raised his hands. Cowden immediately pulled his own gun, and stepped forward to take Sam's. He stepped back again, and motioned for Sam to remount. Sam had a momentary notion to give the pony the spurs, but the gunman at the tree still stood very carefully with the gun at his shoulder. He saw Cowden turn to Tonía and take her hand.

"I'm sorry this had to happen, Tonía. I wish you and your father had kept faith with me. But I'll do all I can to break the agreement you signed."

Tonía said nothing. She continued to look up at Sam with hurt in her dark eyes.

Sam said: "Tonía, if you'll let me. . . ."

Cowden snapped: "You've done your share of talking around here, my friend."

A stable boy had brought his horse, and he swung up.

The gunman by the tree walked over, and Cowden guarded Sam while the other man, a tall, heavy-shouldered American dressed in the California style, mounted his horse.

As they turned to ride, Sam heard Tonía call softly: "*Qué Dios le de justicia.* God give you justice." He could take that two ways, but the way he preferred to take it gave him a little lift of hope.

IV

"LONG-LOOP RODEO"

They rode two miles, with Sam in the lead. Cowden said: "Pull up under that tree." Under a live oak Sam was made to dismount. The big American in the leather vest and tight *charro pantalones* stood near him with his carbine held in the crook of his arm. Cowden had called him Chantry.

Cowden told him to get behind Sam. He stood there with a Colt on the prisoner while Chantry did so. Suddenly Sam's arms were pinioned. Now he began to understand what Will Cowden's agreement breaking would mean.

Cowden balanced on the balls of his feet, standing close to him. "Have you got that paper?"

"No."

Cowden smashed at his jaw, rocking his head with the impact. His eyes were wider, and he sounded breathless. "Now have you got it?"

Sam's lips pressed together tightly. He remained silent.

"We've got too many wise Yankees around this town," Cowden declared. "This is how I'm telling you to leave and not come back."

His fist hit Sam's mouth with a flat smack. Sam began

to fight, but the big man, Chantry, gave his arms a twist that caused him to cry out. Cowden began slugging with both fists. Sam was able to duck some of the blows, but when one landed, it had a stunning force. He felt blood streaming from his mashed lips. He was no longer conscious of pain—everything seemed to be occurring in slow motion.

Then came a shattering force against his head. The dancing figure of the lawyer reeled out of focus, and a soundless dusk closed about him. . . .

He seemed to be riding on a wave of discomfort, which broke then and dumped him miserably on the cold beach of consciousness. He sat for some time against the tree, hearing no sound in the night. He was aware of a crying thirst. He got up, went to his knees, but rose again and held a branch of the tree until his head cleared. At the moment he had no thought of Cowden. He was entirely concerned with the sad plight of Sam Ware. He found his horse not far away, and rode until he found a stream. He lay on the bank for a while, bathing his face. Then he turned over to lie on his back and gaze at the black night sky.

Easy money. Probably more martyrs had died in its name than in that of religion. If this was easy money, he'd take his the hard way. Yet it was hard to see himself riding to San Pedro and taking a boat north. He had a natural reluctance to be bullied out of anything. But it was not this stubbornness that set his compass again toward Rancho San Rafael. It was the look in a girl's eyes when she heard him accused of planning to cheat her.

He would explain. Tell her everything, make her understand that General Tate didn't want to rob them, but to make them prosperous and ride to prosperity with them.

He'd make her believe that, even if he could not quite believe it himself.

He reached the ranch late, turned his horse into the corral, and stumbled into the house. It seemed unreasonably dark. There was a pinpoint of light moving toward him from the end of a long corridor, and now, as he came close, he saw the face of Tonía highlighted behind it. Then this light died, and he knew that the darkness was in his head. He was falling again, with her cry echoing down a long hall to him: "Sam!"

He awoke after a long sleep. Sunlight made a bright square on the wall at the foot of his bed. There was a residue of pain in his head, but other than this he was conscious only of the boundless luxury of lying in such a bed on such a morning.

Someone knocked on the door. Tonía entered, and stood uncertainly by the door. Sam sat up. When she saw that he was all right, she said quickly: "I'll have breakfast sent to you."

"Breakfast in bed," Sam said. "Is that my sentence for lying to you?" When she started for the door, he called her back. "I want to talk to you, Tonía."

"How many more lies do you think will explain this?" She stood close to the bed with her hands clenched. She was small and fragile in the flowered print dress she wore.

"I didn't lie to you, Tonía. Only I didn't tell you all there was to tell. I've got a partner. He asked me to act as his agent because there was some local prejudice against him."

"Against cattle thieves," Tonía said, "there usually is. *Señor* Cowden told me of your partner. Do you know where

35

he got the money to buy your share of San Rafael? With cattle stolen on this ranch he shipped north!"

It came to Sam that Tate's Nevada cattle story might be a lie, after all, but he wasn't going into that until he was sure. He asked her: "How long has Cowden kept books for you?"

"A long time. Why?"

"Because the books for the last two years show that he hasn't accounted for several thousand dollars. In another year, my guess is he'd have offered to lend you the money to get out of debt. And that would have been the end. Unless he took a safer way of grabbing San Rafael. That's what Tate thinks he intends to do. Marry the ranch. It's been done before."

He saw the color come into her face, then she stamped her foot. "If there is a *gringo* in California with manners not fit for a goat herd, I haven't met him."

Sam's laughter followed her.

Later that morning, he sought Guerrero in his office. The old man was reading poetry and sipping wine. Sam stood there some time, and then cleared his throat. Guerrero continued to read. He said quietly: "I do not hear you."

Sam waited a moment longer, and went out into the yard. He felt the quiet pulse of the ranch; servants went to and fro lazily. *Vaqueros* lounged in the shade of a pepper tree, smoking, while one of them strummed a guitar. The ranch was beginning to yaw once more, rudderless, devoid of a steering hand. Suddenly angry, Sam shouted: *"¡Vengan aquí! ¡Que no se sientan por los nalgudos!"*

They came truculently. Sam told Montes, the foreman: "Have the men saddled and ready to ride in fifteen minutes.

Bring food for a week."

Montes hesitated, glanced toward the house, and touched his forehead in deference.

For six days Sam kept them at the rodeo, cleaning up the Noche Buena pasture and moving across the hills to the Corrizo pasture. He stood in a dozen corrals, watching the *fierro* raise smoke from red-brown hides and bloody tabs from ear marks drop into a rawhide sack. When they rode back to San Rafael one night, dusty, unshaven, and exhausted, he had cleaned up a third of the tally and was sure he had not missed two percent of the cattle.

He forced a conference with the Guerreros in the gloomy little office. "Thirty-two hundred animals," he announced. "Half of them ready for sale. In fact, they'll have to be sold if we're to have any graze next year."

Guerrero's dim eyes remained on his face. "Thirty-two hundred. It is surprising." He glanced at the figures Sam had drawn up. "Five hundred cattle in Piedras Negras pasture. Montes made a rough count there last month, to see how much feed we would have to buy. There were seven hundred at that time." He murmured—"*¡'Noches!*"—ironically, and left the room.

Sam sat staring at his figures. "Vicente kept track, too." He frowned. "We agreed to within twenty cows."

"He doesn't question your count," Tonía said. "He only questions what happened to the other two hundred cattle. I suppose he wonders what your partner was doing while you had all the men on the roundup on Noche Buena."

She left the room. Sam went over the count again, and suddenly the words jumped out at him. Piedras Negras! It was near Piedras Negras that he was to meet Tate and talk over their plans.

He sat there through two cigarettes, thinking about his partner and companion, General George Tate. Shrewd but honest, he had claimed. But stealing two hundred cows exceeded shrewdness. Perhaps the fifty steers he had sold at Nevada City had come from the same pasture.

In his room, Sam extracted the loads from his Dragoon Colt and replaced them with fresh powder. For the interview that was ahead, he wanted no misfires. It was eight o'clock when he left the ranch. He crossed the bridge at a race and swung toward the trail across the hills.

The mountain trail was a narrow defile cut through dry, tangled growth higher than his head, whispering with the sounds of nocturnal animals. From the summit he looked down on a dark pattern of intersecting valleys.

Directly below, a light made a soft puddle of flame on the shore of the Piedras Negras pasture. It was too big a fire to denote a line rider's campfire, and it told Sam in an instant what was going on.

He rode down. In a sparse oak grove at the edge of the valley, he could hear the crackling of fires. A sickening odor of spoiling carcasses struck him. He rode to the edge of the camp and leaned on the swell of the saddle to watch a dozen shirtless men at work among the fires.

Great iron kettles suspended on tripods hung above the fires. Beef carcasses boiled in them, giving off a stinking vapor. Two Mexicans with skinning knives were butchering a carcass hung from a tree. In the middle of it all—passing down an aisle of tallow barrels, laying a possessive hand on bales of half-cured hides—came General Tate, sweat gleaming redly on his naked belly and face, blood on his hands and trousers.

He stopped where two men were skinning tallow from one of the kettles into a barrel. Then his eyes raised, and

Sam saw him start a little as he tried to decide whether it was really a horseman he saw beyond the light, or just a shadow.

"A SHIP IN THE HARBOR"

Sam rode in, and swung down. "Howdy, General. Keeping busy, I see."

Tate's big, rutted face captured an overly hearty smile. "By George, I looked for you yesterday, boy!"

"You sure didn't look for me tonight," Sam drawled.

Tate's hand airily indicated the bustling camp. "Got that boat to meet me on the Twenty-Seventh," he declared. "No use letting grass grow under my feet. Whatever I get for the hides and tallow, of course, I'll split with old Guerrero."

"Of course," Sam said.

Tate gave him a pinched glance, and then he wiped his hands on his trousers. "How'd it go? Any trouble?"

Sam said: "Not until Cowden came up and spilled it that we'd jumped him."

"Hell, didn't you tell him what we found out about him?"

"Yes, but he happened to mention that you were wanted for cow stealing. So how did that make me look, when I had to admit I was in partnership with you?"

Tate stared at him. "You didn't swallow that yarn?"

"I didn't know whether to swallow it or not. But tonight I decided to find out, after the count ran two hundred steers short in this area. I reckon this settles it."

Tate's face suddenly writhed. He seized the other's arm. "I want none of your lollygagging preachments! You wanted easy money, and I told you I'd give you some. But you were afraid of getting your lace cuffs soiled. Get it through your head that there ain't easy money around these days without a risk tied onto it."

Sam stared into his face, and Tate let his hand fall away and cooled down a trifle. "I'm sorry you had to find out before you were ready for it, Sam. In time you will be. I make no mistake about that. About the thirty thousand . . . I aim to let Guerrero ranch just about the way he wants to. I'll keep busy on the side, like now. Sooner or later, he's bound to go under. When he does, it'll be my money that buys the ranch, and I'll be paying most of it to myself. And that'll just be the start."

"No," Sam said. "It won't even be that, because it's going to end right here. The money is still in the safe. I'll bring it back to you. Then we'll break it off clean."

Tate's shoulder made a rolling motion, and, before Sam could duck, his fist struck him on the cheek bone and sent him foundering back. He gathered himself quickly and faced Tate as the general came forward, shouting: "You wanted to be a preacher, eh? By God, I'll make an angel out of you! I'll not be eased out of this game by any simpering dandy."

He came in recklessly. Sam took his time, fending off three wild swings before he gathered all his fury in one overhand blow that exploded in the middle of Tate's face. Tate came up on his toes like a man who has taken a bullet in the back. He stretched both hands before him, staring blindly at Sam. Sam watched him crash heavily to the ground. It was his first moment of triumph in many days.

The Mexicans among the fires were starting for him.

Sam legged it to his pony, sprang into the saddle, and left at a lope.

He reached San Rafael after midnight. A plan to duck anything Tate might throw at him was shaping up in his mind. He entered the house, traversed the parlor and hall to his room. As he placed his hand on the wrought-iron latch, the hood of a lantern grated, and a beam of light impaled him against the door.

Tonía laughed lightly at his shock. "Did you forget others can work at night, too?"

She came from beside a carved chest at the end of the hall. She was dressed in a dark gown, her hair undone and falling down her back. Sam leaned against the wall, watching her set the lamp in a window ledge.

She spoke again bitterly: "You Yankees are so efficient. Something like shame, or pity, never stops you from doing something you want to. Did you find the cattle, Sam . . . or did you lose another two hundred?"

Sam said: "Will you believe me if I explain where I was?"

"A *californio*," Tonía said, "will believe anything."

Sam's patience snapped. "I've been stealing cattle all right," he said. "And here's something else I've been wanting to do!"

She gasped as he caught her wrist and pulled her toward him. His arm captured her waist. He had expected her to fight, but there was little resistance, and she came up hard against him, with Sam raising her off the floor as he kissed her.

There was an instant of victory, but it died quickly. She had stolen his triumph by submitting to him. The scent, the warm presence of her, seemed to fill him

41

and yet to be unattainable. . . .

He put her down. "Tonía," he said, "I. . . ."

Suddenly he saw that she was no longer mocking. There was a softness in her eyes. "You're sorry? I'm not, Sam. It's the first thing you've told me that I could believe. And now I want to believe everything."

From somewhere in the dark house an old man's voice called inquiringly: "Tonía?"

Tonía put a finger on his lips. *"Que deurmase bien."* He watched her take the lantern, and move down the corridor to her own room.

In the morning Sam heard breakfast dishes rattling in the kitchen before he was up. He dressed and entered the warm reek of *huevos rancheros* and coffee in the big dining room. Guerrero was at the head of the great table, a grizzled, saber-nosed old vulture whose eyes did not welcome the Yankee. But Sam sat down and saw Tonía's eyes avoid his but her lips play with a smile.

Guerrero arose presently, without finishing.

Sam said: *"Don* Bonifacio, I've got to talk to you."

"Why?"

"Because you're being robbed of ten or twenty cattle a night while you sit around mooning about the old days," Sam said. "We've got to work fast for the next few days, and you'll have to work with me."

"You seem capable of working without me," the Mexican remarked.

Tonía spoke sharply: "Father, we've listened to everything *Señor* Cowden had to say about him, but we haven't let him talk for himself. After all, what is Will Cowden but a Yankee?"

Guerrero sat down, staring at her. "A change of heart?"

he inquired suspiciously. "But he hasn't denied yet that he tricked us about his partner."

"No," Sam said, "because I believed the story he told me. But I paid him a surprise visit last night. He was butchering cattle for the hides and tallow. There's nothing we can do about it except beat him to the punch when he tries to ship them."

The *ranchero*'s dim eyes kept studying Sam's face, reserving their judgment. "And how do we do that?"

"There's nothing to prevent you from working the same trick Tate did," Sam told him. "Even these half-starved cattle are worth fancy prices in northern California. Tate got the money to buy in with you by stealing your cattle and shipping them north. This Captain Morrissey goes to Baja, California and cuts wild hay. The animals are probably jammed into the hold so they can't move. All they can do is eat and put on fat. We've got four or five days before the ship is due, but it will take three days to get them there."

"And what if Tate reaches the harbor at the same time you do?" Tonía asked.

Sam frowned. "Then I'll have to talk him out of shipping anything. And it may not be only Tate. If I know him, he'll tie up with Cowden to fight us. He'll make an asset out of a liability every time." Then he said: "*Don* Bonifacio, you were talking about a *fiesta*. I think we'll have one, after all." He did not explain why, but he was thinking that it might be the last excuse these people ever found for a *fiesta*. He wasn't going to deny them that much.

For the next three days there was activity. Little strings of cattle trailed down the washes toward a central holding point. Around the *hacienda,* workers dug barbecue pits and hung strings of chilis from the *vigas*. *Vaqueros* from distant line camps began to arrive. Romances that had languished began to flare once more.

On the morning of the *fiesta,* fires began to blaze in the pits as the cooks prepared the deep beds of coals they required to roast the beef carcasses. Through that day the incense of burning oak hung over the ranch. The *fiesta* would begin at dusk and last all night and the next day.

At four o'clock a rider arrived from the hills above the ranch. He sought Guerrero, who spoke to Montes, the *mayordomo.* Then all three of them came to Sam. The rider was a slender Mexican youth called Feliciano. He carried an old sea glass Sam had found on the place. Sam had sent him out the day the roundup started.

"*Patrón,*" he said, "this morning I am watching the harbor, as you instructed me. I see a ship of many sails drop anchor."

Sam frowned. The old *Mary E.* was ahead of schedule. He had hoped the *fiesta* would be over before they must start. He said hurriedly: "Pick twelve of your best men, Montes. If we ride all night, we may make it by sunup."

VI

"BLOOD IN THE BAY"

While the *fiesta* was beginning in the patio, riders began to assemble among the trees. They sat casually on home-made wooden saddles with ponchos thrown carelessly over their shoulders while Sam told them briefly what to expect.

Guerrero came from the dusk on his big gray stallion. Sam had not expected him. He tried to ease the old man out as tactfully as he could.

"I was thinking it might be better for you to stay here. If anything happens at the ranch, you ought to be on hand."

Guerrero snorted. "You learn to speak like a Mexican. What you mean is that I am so old I would be in the way. If I am that ancient, my friend, I hope I may not come back from the fight."

Sam gave up. They picked up the day herd at the river, with the three men who guarded it. They took it down the dry bed of the river, passing through the edge of the pueblo around midnight. They stopped once, letting the herd water in the mossy trickle of water down the middle of the wash while the *vaqueros* munched *panoja* and drank wine from leather bags. A cold slice of moon was rising. About three, Sam asked Guerrero how much farther it was.

"Maybe seven miles," the Mexican said.

"That will bring us to the harbor by dawn. I'll cut ahead and try to arrange things with the captain."

He rode up the shelving bank to the rolling rangeland above. Hills prevented any view of the ocean in the thin moonlight, but somewhere, Sam suspected, General George Tate moved along behind a herd with his capable eye out for whatever obstacle developed. There was a possibility that he had already made the harbor. However, Sam suspected he, too, had been unprepared for the ship's early return. Yet, if the loading of his steers had begun, there would be no alternative but a gunfight.

In the still hour of dawn, he reached the summit of a knoll and saw the sleeping harbor below him, the waves booming distantly on the surf. The high strakes and slim masts of the *Mary E.* were etched like steel points against a gray sea.

Sam turned to search the hills and saw no sign of another herd. He rode down the hill to the beach. A rowboat was drawn up beyond a brine tank in which hides were curing. He saw no one about, and ran it into the still water and took the oars.

As he approached the schooner, the voice of Captain Morrissey boomed out above him: "You're down early, young fellow."

Sam rested on the oars and looked up at the blue-coated, white-haired figure of the master. The sun, just rising, was on his face, and Sam caught the flash of his cheap store teeth.

"I have a cargo for you, Captain," he called up. "Two hundred steers, or all you can ship of them."

Morrissey sounded faintly amused. "It's still the earliest bird gets the worm, Ware. Your friend was here last night to bespeak his own cargo. Hides, tallow, and steers. They'll be along today. I couldn't jam another pound of cargo aboard with a bootjack."

"How does he pay you?" Sam demanded. "A split, or by weight?"

"I'm not sure that concerns you," Morrissey declared.

"I was wondering," Sam told him, "whether you're making enough to warrant the risk you take."

Morrissey studied him. "I'm not aware of taking any risk."

"Do you know what the punishment is for piracy in California? They impound the boat and sometimes impound the master for a few years. There hasn't been much of it lately, but I don't think they'd like to see it start again. Tate's bringing you a cargo of stolen cattle. If you take it, I'll be in San Francisco to meet you when you dock. I'll be with the port authorities, and, if you don't have papers on those animals, you'll find you'll do your sailing behind bars for a while."

46

Morrissey's face was stony, but he could not keep alarm out of his voice. "A lot of cargo is barter. If I tried to carry papers on everything. . . ."

"Then I'll put it this way . . . will you carry my cattle or his? The owner of my herd is with me. He also owns the herd Tate's bringing."

Morrissey raised his eyes to the hills behind the harbor. He studied them a while. "What will you pay?"

"Double the regular rate."

Morrissey mulled it over. He said, sounding disgruntled: "They'll have to be loaded by sling. Bring them across the shallows so they won't have so far to swim." He vanished from the rail.

Sam rode back. He had only passed the first rank of hills when he saw, screaming across a ridge a half mile to the north, a brown flood of cattle moving in swirling dust, their horns flashing. He came down from the crest so that he would not be so readily visible, lingering to count the riders who moved along beside and behind the herd. He discerned the figures of at least a dozen horsemen.

A couple of miles behind came Guerrero's herd, rising from the streambed to the range and beginning to wind through a narrow pass in the hills. Sam found Guerrero and Montes.

"They're going to beat us. Tate's brought a herd, all right. But I've jockeyed the captain into taking our herd instead of his. Tate can't get his cattle aboard if they won't let down the slings. All we can do is hope he'll give up and let us ship ours."

They brought the herd down through the hills to the tide flats. The cattle moved slowly through the tough salt grass, their hoofs sucking in the marsh. Beyond were the whitewashed sheds and houses of the hide curers, rosy in the early light, and past them the harbor was still veiled in pearly mist.

The sea was a gray plain, its surf tossing restlessly against the cliffs. It was all too quiet, too peaceful, to be a setting for bloodshed. Down at the side of the boat the heads of cattle showed like pronged corks, the *vaqueros* walking their horses through the shallows behind them.

Sam perceived that there was trouble. Many of the cattle were trying to turn back, while on a spit that ran along the channel General George Tate stood in the stirrups to shout something through cupped hands at the boat. Some of the cowpunchers hesitated, and turned back. A horse that had carried its rider nearly to the ship turned and came lunging up the beach. Tate must have given an order, for now all the riders returned, leaving the cattle swimming aimlessly in the harbor.

Sam saw him draw a carbine and take a bead on the ship. But in a moment he jammed the gun back in the boot, and turned disgustedly to confront the hills. As he did so, he saw the Guerrero herd moving across the salt-crusted flats.

Sam spoke quickly to the Mexican. "Keep them coming."

He rode ahead, and stopped a hundred feet from where the cowpunchers were congregating on the beach. Now he could make out the figure of Cowden and the big-shouldered bulk of Chantry. He had figured Tate's strategy correctly—Tate had allied with an old enemy to fight a new one.

Sam raised his arm. "I want a parley, General."

Tate rode out, and reined in his pony fifteen feet away, stony, flint-eyed, breathing hard.

"Better find a new game," Sam said. "We're taking those cattle to the mines. Guerrero will return your money. But you're not ranching any more."

Tate's profane oratory lasted for some time. It finally dwindled into savage invective. "You cowardly whelp," he snarled. "So now it's you thinks you're going to marry a ranch, eh? Maybe I can fix that, too."

"I may," Sam admitted. "But the ranch is just a coincidence. All that concerns you, Tate, is that you and I never heard of each other. I'm shipping a herd of cattle. What you do is your own business."

Tate said slowly: "You're not taking a herd of cattle anywhere. I dealt you into this. You'll cut me in for my share or you'll finish your cattle drive right here." Tate's forehead wrinkled with a hard wink. "A third of it, Sam," he said tensely. "I'll meet you at Nevada City and manage the whole thing. I'll milk them for enough that you'll make more than if you sold them yourself."

Sam shook his head. "We're just ranchers, General, not cardsharps. It's no deal. I'm sorry you and I had to break up, but it took you to convince me that I didn't want easy money so much as I wanted to be able to look other men in the eye. I want to show this old galoot that there's at least one square Yankee in California." Then he put out his hand. "So long, General."

Tate's mouth pursed, and he spat so accurately that Sam had to jerk his hand away to avoid the spittle. But he only laughed as Tate swung his horse violently and rode back to his men.

The cattle were beginning to bawl as they hit the water. Cowboys yelled and swung their plaited rawhide ropes, crowding them into the shallows. Sam joined Vicente, the corporal, at the point. All the men had drawn saddle guns

49

and rode with more attention on Tate's crowd than on the cattle. Tate was conferring with Cowden. Presently they turned and started from the beach. They rode up the long slope of a hill.

Guerrero exhaled his breath. "*Grac' a Dios.* They will not fight us."

Sam grunted, watching the band of riders disappear over the ridge. Tate, he thought, was decidedly out of character. A feeling of uneasiness continued to ride him as they waded deeper into the water, and suddenly he said: "Four of the men can handle the herd. Tate's too good a field marshal to give up that easily. We're going to be ready if he comes back."

Guerrero appeared annoyed. "But, *hombre* . . . *!*"

Sam said sharply: "If you want your horse shot out from under you, in twenty feet of water, with your boots and shell belts to sink you, go ahead. I'm going to have sand under me."

Guerrero's shoulders gave reluctant assent. They left the horses in a plank corral behind the shacks, and Sam stood, trying to decide where he would bring a force if he were attempting a coup such as he suspected Tate had in mind. He decided it would be down the same shallow cañon where he had brought the herd. He led them to the wind-riffled dunes at the mouth of the cañon. Purple verbena carpeted the sand ridges. There was little shelter, however, and he stood searching for a point of vantage.

It was while he stood there that the abrupt drumming of hoofs in sand came to him. He shouted a warning, and dropped to one knee. He had figured everything but the time element. Tate had brought his gang back on a hard lope. They were spurring up the sand to the ridge where Sam's *vaqueros* stood bunched in suicidal deployment. Sam saw them through the peep sight of his carbine, coming like a flung spear, slashing hard at the *vaqueros* frantically trying to dig in for the shock. Tate had found them and was shouting his men on.

Sam let the hammer of his carbine fall, and the gun jolted against his shoulder. The Mexican riding at the point came up on his toes, flinging his arms to the sky. His horse began to shy. He went down in the sand, rolling over and over to the bottom of the slope.

Other guns were crashing, but the shots went off hastily. Sam worked the lever of his rifle, and the shell left the chamber in a shining arc. He tried to slip another cartridge home, but now the horses were plowing over the ridge. Two or three men went sprawling down the slope. Deafeningly the thunder of revolvers broke against his ears.

He lay flat on the sand. He had a terrifying glimpse of Tate, riding past, spurring his mount over him, and leaning from the saddle to fire straight down. The bullet struck the sand in the middle of the C that Sam's body made. The hoofs of the horse beat the earth beside him, one thudding against his boot, wrenching his foot and tearing the heel from the boot.

Vicente lay on the sand with blood pouring sluggishly from a wound in his head. Another man lay on his side, clutching his belly, but the rest were getting dazedly to their feet as Tate brought his men about to charge them before they could get set. He was riding back up, more slowly this time because of the steep slope. He would be returning for the kill. He slipped the shell into the chamber of the rifle and started down the slope.

Then Sam heard boots in the sand behind him, and saw old Bonifacio Guerrero take his place ten feet away, at his left. He looked stiff and tense, but in his hand he held a pistol his grandfather must have owned—a double-barreled side-hammer with the bore of a cannon.

Sam brought his gun up. He saw a pale burst of flame from the muzzle of Tate's Colt, but the gun was fired without care. Sam settled his feet. In his sights was a wedge of pleated shirt above the man's tight-buttoned frock coat, and he had a moment's recollection of a day long ago when he had admired that fancy shirt and the man who wore it. He saw the tiny hole punctured in the shirt, just below the second button. Then he saw that all the life, the vitality and exuberance, had sloughed from Tate's face. It was a dead face he looked at, a face rutted with old sins. It looked on Sam without comprehension, then blood rushed from the mouth, and Sam looked away.

He dropped the carbine. He heard Guerrero fire his pistol once, then again to empty the second barrel. He saw Cowden grab at the neck of his horse.

Chantry was the first to break. He turned his horse, but the others crowded him, and there was a tangle. Chantry took a bullet in the back. Someone shouted—"¡Amigo! ¡Amigo!"—raising his hands. There was a spatter of firing from Guerrero's cowpunchers, which ended as hands began to rise. Cowden was down, Tate lay on the sand, and the cavalier spirit that had brought his men to the harbor was now a torn pennant on a shattered lance.

Sam let the others take charge of rounding up the prisoners. He wanted to get away from the smell of powder and death.

It was mid-afternoon when they finished loading the cattle. Sam prepared to row out to the ship in the longboat for the trip to San Francisco. He was taking Montes and a few cowpunchers with him. He didn't know how Guerrero

52

felt about a Yankee partner, now, but he gave him a chance to say as the old man came up.

"You'll have your men and your money back in a month," he told him. "I'll get the best price I can and send the money back with Montes."

Guerrero frowned. "Why with Montes?"

"Someday," Sam told him, "I'll come back to see Tonía. But it will be as a guest. It was Tate's money that bought the partnership, and Tate is dead. It's all yours. But I'll give you some advice. Never trust a Yankee again unless he's wearing a halo."

The old man looked through him. "We are talking foolishness. I have a ranch, without the understanding to run it. Furthermore, I have a daughter who will leave me if I come back with any such nonsense. About a month, then, *hijo mío?*"

Hijo mío—my son. In Sam's heart, the ice began to melt. It was going to be all right—all right with the old man, all right with the girl. That was about all he could ask. He gripped Guerrero's hand, and smiled.

"Maybe three weeks," he said.

The Last Mustang

It seemed to Wild-Horse Farnum that a man who was partial to a particular horse was in the position of a tuba player: He must drag the danged thing with him wherever he went. Wild-Horse was partial to two horses, a knot-headed steeldust and a little pack animal with no foolishness about him.

Farnum liked to travel in style, so he engaged an emigrant car at Denver, gave the horses the rear portion, and boarded in the front. Three days later, he and the horses were set down at a water tank in southern Utah, on a green prairie sliding up to an austere range of mountains. He stood and gaped at them the way a gold-rush miner might have gaped at a beautiful woman.

The ghost of a snowy peak floated above the purple crests. He thought of early summer freshets singing between banks of willow and aspen, of trout, and bands of wild ponies waiting to be trapped. Something like a hairspring in him began to oscillate.

Wild-Horse Farnum needed mountains as an ouzel needs water. They were his religion; they were his belief in the hereafter. In the mountains he had been born; to the mountains he would return when these mustanging and bronc'-stomping days were over. He thought of them as a little like himself—big, spectacular, and lonely.

In the shade of the water tower, he packed one horse and saddled the other, swung his lemon-yellow chaps into the saddle, and started for the mountains. He had been curious about these mountains ever since passing them in another emigrant car another spring. He had vowed to come back and trap in them someday. This year he had made arrangements to do his summer horse trapping in the Whetstone Mountains. By first snow, he would have his brand on a good herd of canners, worthless, cold-blooded grass stealers with a leavening of perhaps a dozen ponies to be trained and sold as saddlers. And he would know about those mountains.

A fresh cattle trail led him into the foothills. At a town called Council City he was to meet several ranchers to whom he had written about the possibility of trapping in their mountain range. Near sundown, he was about to give up hope of making Council City by dark, when he smelled juniper smoke and heard a wild cowboy yell. He decided he had caught up with the herd he had been following. This was at a gap in some low hills tufted like a candlestick bedspread. Wild-Horse reset his sombrero over his right eye and got the horse into a showy single foot, as an actor might swallow a lozenge before his entrance. Entrances were everything to him.

Everything about Wild-Horse Farnum was big—his hands, his heart, and his loneliness. He played the part of a one-man Wild West show, but always he would peer at himself doubtfully from various angles in an attempt to see how he looked to other people. The lemon-yellow chaps, silk shirt, and white Stetson were the greasepaint of a magnificent ham actor who was his own best audience. His histrionics brought him many acquaintances, but he had never quite made a friend. His soul dwelt apart from all the noise, small and abashed.

A rider came toward him through the gap. His entrance thus spoiled, all Wild-Horse could do was to pull and raise his hand shoulder high, saying: "Howdy! I'm Wild-Horse Farnum."

He thought the man smiled, although it was too dark to be sure. He was rangy and solemn, plainly dressed in brush-popper jacket, jeans, and work chaps. His Stetson was raw-edged and flat, and a shadow hung from the brim.

"Howdy," he said. "I'm Shevlin. I ramrod for C. Y. Moss."

They shook hands.

Wild-Horse expected to ride on and have supper with the cowboys, perhaps yarn a bit, but Shevlin said: "You might as well throw off here. Nothing flat enough to bed a wood tick up yonder. We've ate and set guards. I'll bunk with you here."

Wild-Horse knew he was being put off. He was not unduly curious, however. He saw many strange things in his poking into the remote pigeonholes of the back country. He let Shevlin's terse explanation suffice for the time: "We're bringin' a little herd down to the railroad."

In the morning, the herd had drifted considerably south. The mustanger's way was north. "See you up yonder, anyhow," Wild-Horse Farnum told Shevlin.

"Not on Moss's land," Shevlin retorted.

"How come?"

The ramrod's lanky shoulders rose and dropped. "Ask him. I only work here." He rode after the herd drifting deeper into the hills.

Wild-Horse Farnum was bothered. When he trapped, he did not like to worry about artificial things like boundaries. It was awkward to pull up in the middle of a broncho chase because you were on the wrong ranch. He would have to hooraw this man, C. Y. Moss, into line.

* * * * *

His first vista of Council City caught at his heart. The only thing he had seen to compare with the village was an Alpine hamlet on a lumberyard calendar. Peaked roofs and a church spire poked through a green froth of trees. A creek bisected the town. Behind, the mountains lifted their magnificent heads.

For years he had been searching for such a town. Not to settle in, but to remember in case he ever got too crippled or too old to mustang and wanted a place where he could dig in. Wild-Horse liked his way of life too well to stop moving before he had to. He loved horses, and he liked to hit a town dramatically, tell the ranchers how it was going to be, and trail into the thunderous crags most men hesitated to cross afoot let alone on horseback after a band of wild horses. He grew fat on applause. His chief night fear was of sinking into the obscuring mud of a prosaic life.

His round-robin letter had said he would be in Council City on the Eighth, when most of the cattlemen would be in town for the spring roping. It was not quite noon when he arrived. Streamers fluttered up and down the main street. Horses and turnouts thronged the road, children and dogs darting perilously among them. Wild-Horse's histrionic soul leaped up like a dog with dirty feet—all the elements of drama were here for a man who knew how to mix them.

He rode as far as the hotel when, suddenly, the steeldust appeared to shy. Wild-Horse lost the come-along of the pack horse, and both horses went to pitching. His sombrero sailed away; his chaps flapped like yellow wings. A cowboy shouted: "Powder River! Let 'er buck!"

There in the street it was touch-and-go with Wild-Horse Farnum for a while. The horse was pitching fence-cornered, coming down on stiff legs with a jarring power that snapped the mustang's neck like the popper of a whip. Shaking his head, the pony rattled the silver-mounted bridle and bit. In the middle of it, Wild-Horse blew a stirrup, and after two more lunges landed on his hip pockets in the road.

The crowd rocked with laughter at the sight.

He got up slowly, wiped his nose, and stared at the big stallion. Then, warily, he moved toward it. He recovered the reins and vaulted back in the saddle, spurring savagely with the sides of his boots. For a full minute, the broncho bucked from one side of the road to the other—responding to the secret language they had whenever he came too near a child—but at the end of that time he stood still, refusing to buck. Balkily he moved to a hitch rack.

Wild-Horse slid to the ground. Recovering his Stetson, he said darkly: "There, golhorn you! No bronc' is gonna pitch me just because he's got used to ridin' boxcars and thinks he's better'n me!" His glance moved to the grinning crowd. "Boys," he said, "I'm Wild-Horse Farnum. Can anybody direct me to C. Y. Moss?"

A stocky, middle-aged man in worn bib overalls regarded him loweringly: "I'm Moss. It's no dice . . . even after that free rodeo."

Farnum winked at a girl in the crowd. "Can we talk some place?"

The hotel lobby was no better, no worse, than most cowtown lobbies. The furniture was spur-marked like a rodeo bucker. The floor was unswept, and a rubber mat under an almost pristine cuspidor was festooned with hits. Three men went inside with Farnum. The girl he had winked at also trailed along, a pretty girl with hair the color of oak shavings. She wore a dark skirt and a sentimental sort of white shirtwaist with a red ribbon worked through the open material at throat and wrists. She didn't look like the kind of girl who would trail men around hotel lobbies, however.

"Young lady,"—Wild-Horse smiled—"we're pretty rough-talking *hombres*. Why don't you go out to the fair-grounds and have a candied apple?"

"I'll keep my hands close to my ears," she said.

The tall mustanger shrugged and turned to C. Y. Moss. "What's the matter, you don't want your range curried of no-account horses so you can raise decent stock?"

"I let some fellers trap on my ranch once," Moss growled. "I had three forest fires and lost my best brood mare." Moss was a pounded-down-looking rancher, his bib overalls bleached and patched, his face harried, red, and pitted with lines. He smoked a pale green cigar.

"When did you ever let anybody trap on your ranch?" the girl demanded.

Color pushed angrily through C. Y. Moss's face. Wild-Horse, too, was irritated. Let this thing go much further, and he never would josh the man into line. "Maybe we can talk in the saloon," he suggested.

The girl sat down. "No use. I'd go in the family entrance, anyway. After all, I run more cattle than Moss. I'm Brink."

"Brink!" Farnum had thought S. Brink, who owned the Fiddleback Ranch, must be Sam, or Syrus, or something.

"Susan," she said. "Sit down, Wild-Horse. I'm all for you. I'm sick of my mares bringing their darned roach-backed, coon-footed colts down for me to feed. What's your deal?"

Off balance, Wild-Horse groped for the stirrups and finally started out: "Why . . . I figure I earn the bronc's I catch. Fact is, I usually find folks glad to lend me a few unbroke horses to use for the work. I've never started a fire in a hotel lobby or a saloon, so why should I start one in the mountains? I wouldn't hardly spit on the ground, even, because the mountains are home to me. All unbranded horses go to me, except colts with branded mares. That's my deal."

"Good enough. You can start any time you want."

A big, pallid-looking rancher named Whitten had been watching Wild-Horse closely. He seemed to reach a decision. "Ain't that a little one-sided? The cannery must pay you seven, eight a head. You can trap my range, but I'll want ten percent of your gross."

Wild-Horse found himself hurt and cheated by the whole interview. He had been received like any mustanger who might come through unannounced. They hadn't even commented on his riding. His impulse was to agree to the ten percent and get on up. Temperamentally he was unfitted for dickering. A man who likes to be liked cannot drive a great bargain.

Susan Brink sniffed. "That's ridiculous, Whit. You wouldn't risk your neck that way for all the seven-dollar bronc's in Utah. Don't you give him a cent, Wild-Horse."

Whitten colored like a boy caught writing a naughty word on the blackboard. Backed up, Wild-Horse said: "I wasn't going to. It's a straight deal, Mister Whitten."

Whitten laughed. "OK, then. I'm outnumbered."

C. Y. Moss arose tartly, dropping his cigar on the floor. "For ten percent or for fifty, you won't trap a horse on my ranch. It's above my bend to make a living on that ranch, anyhow! One of these days"—he said, looking straight at the Brink girl—"I'm going after what's rightly mine. Then maybe I can afford forest fires and stolen stock like other folks."

Wild-Horse made an observation. "You talk poor but

you smoke rich, Moss. If I could afford stogies like the one you just threw away, I wouldn't be wearing patched overalls."

It was an inconsequential remark, but it hit Moss like a mule's hind hoof. He looked down at the greenish cigar. He opened his mouth, shut it, stared turgidly a moment, and departed.

Wild-Horse completed his arrangements with the other ranchers and found himself alone with Susan Brink on the boardwalk before the hotel. He felt immeasurably better. A little strut was coming back to his legs. "You might as well start work up my way," Susan told him. "It's at the south end, and you can work north. I've got a carry-all. You can haul your groceries as far as the place before you pack. We'll see the show and go up tomorrow."

In the morning, with the mustanger's horses trailing the big yellow carry-all, they headed up a deep-rutted road through green parks sentried with juniper and fir. For Wild-Horse Farnum, it was like a glimpse into a dream—the oft-repeated dream he had had of just such a country, of meadows and mountains, and a valley he had even given a name—Pleasant Valley.

"That was a beautiful ride you made," she said. "Do you always hit a town so dramatically?"

"Seems like Speck gets ornacious every time we move."

"Don't be fooling me, mustanger. You picked that spot because it was the busiest one in the street! But it was still nice."

It was gentle reproof that did not sting. He asked about how she managed with the ranch. "I've been the boss for a couple of years," she told him. "The winters got too rough on Pop. He's down at the Pioneers' Home at Prescott. My foreman runs things for me, except when it takes any thinking."

"What did Moss mean . . . 'things that were rightly his'?"

"That's the skeleton in the closet. There's a little dispute on my place that goes back to Coronado. Nobody ever noticed it until Moss bought in. He's squawked about it ever since. He thinks he owns all my mountain range."

They passed the first ridge and gained a bench where the timber grew stouter. The new summer grass was a bright background for white-faced Hereford cattle.

"Got a wife, Wild-Horse?" Susan asked.

"Nor kids."

"A drifter never amounts to anything until he gets married."

"Drifting's my business."

They emerged from some trees. He saw before him a most glorious panorama. A valley climbed from the trees up a long corridor shaped by steep hills. Behind were the mountains—real mountains you would excuse yourself to when you regurgitated. The valley was like a green inland lake lapping dark, fragrant woods. A creek, capricious as a girl, wound deviously the length of it.

She was watching him. "Isn't it beautiful?"

Some obscure defense mechanism flashed into operation in the mustanger, obscure and perverse, for this was Pleasant Valley, the embodiment of his dream. But it was also a green graveyard of ambitions. Here a man like him would grow prosaic and stodgy. The world would forget him. In ten years, people would laugh at a fat, wheezing cattleman ludicrously nicknamed Wild-Horse Farnum.

"Scenery is scenery," he said offhandedly.

"No scenery in the world is like this," she declared.

They rode on.

At the ranch, a snug lay-out of log cabins and pole corrals, Wild-Horse met Noah Eagleson, the ramrod. Noah was small, brown, and stringy, like a chunk of sunburned gristle. He was entirely captivated by the big, colorful horse trapper with his sauntering ways. That night he cackled over Farnum's stories and card tricks. He said: "Wild-Horse, I've got a bronc' in the trap I'll bet two dollars you can't stay fifteen seconds with!"

In the morning, Wild-Horse topped a hard-bitten grulla for two dollars and some glory. The horse could not buck for sour owl feathers, but he made a pretty ride so the old man would not feel bad. Then he got ready for his first foray into the hills. Noah was proud to go along as his gate man.

"Take a change of clothes," Wild-Horse told him, "and a pair of cotton gloves. Those bronc's smell you, or your hands on the trap, and they're a-goin' to explode in seven different directions."

Susan stood in the yard, smiling encouragement as they rode by, her prettiness glistening like the summer day. When they reached the trees, she waved and cried: "Excelsior!"

Wild-Horse didn't get it, but he waved back.

At timberline, in a gaunt valley choked with boulders and dwarf pines, they built the funnel. It was a camouflaged fence of brush and small trees across a shallow dead-end cañon, with a pole gate easily shut. "Just lay low in the rocks till the horses are inside," Wild-Horse directed. "Then slam the gate. I may be a week."

"How do I know when you're coming?"

"You'll hear us."

Up through the mountains and the wreckage of mountains Wild-Horse rode, driving a mount of four ponies wearing new broncho shoes. This was dangerous and exacting work, and the stoutest of double-cinching was not stout enough. The trees acquired a starved look. The air grew sharp as chilled Rhenish wine. At about eleven thousand feet, Wild-Horse sighted his first band of horses—a dozen mustangs moving along the bottom of a cañon. It was beyond the divide, and he was not sure whose range the horses were in, but he made sure he could run them to where he wanted them before he started down.

He had ridden about halfway down when something exploded startlingly on a rock beside the trail, and he sat looking at a silver streak on the gray granite. Then he heard the echoes of a shot pouring down the cañon. Distantly a man bawled: "Farnum! I'm coming down!" It was the voice of Elmo Shevlin, C. Y. Moss's ramrod.

By George, you better come primed for fight! Wild-Horse raged silently.

In about ten minutes the ramrod rode down the trail. Angrily he dismounted and stalked toward the mustanger. He was a harder-looking man than he had seemed that night by the campfire, all the fat leached from his body by work, the softness from his face by chronic rancor. He was nearly as big as Farnum, wearing jeans and a horsehide jacket over a striped jersey. He strode up menacingly and had his mouth open to bark something when Wild-Horse hit him. Blood started from his nose as from a spigot. He staggered, and sat down on the trail with tears in his eyes and a look of absolute astonishment. Wild-Horse loomed over him. "Do you know how close you came to killing me? Three feet!"

Shevlin found a bandanna and clamped it over his nose.

He had lost his impetus, but retorted defensively: "I could come closer than that. Farnum, we warned you. . . ."

"Yes, and what if I'd moved? Or the bullet'd glanced? You warned me what?" he demanded.

"To keep off the range. You passed Brink's boundary a mile back."

"That's not far." He glanced down the cañon and saw no sign of the horses. In rising anger, he stared at the foreman. "They've blowed. Say, what are you doing over here, that you're so all-fired touchy about trespassers?"

Shevlin was on his feet, trying to find a dry spot on the bandanna. "It ain't me, Wild-Horse. It's the boss. He's edgy about fires since he was burned out that time."

Wild-Horse grunted. "I'm riding down and look for those bronc's. Next time you've got something to say to me, it better come out of that Twenty-Two-caliber mouth instead of a Thirty-Thirty-caliber car-been."

Shevlin said: "OK, OK, Wild-Horse."

Wild-Horse rode on. He had not felt so good since he grand-marshaled the rodeo at Silver City. The horde of little doubts that had besieged him for a week was routed.

For three more weeks he partook of his false confidence. He was no longer afraid of Susan Brink and her beautiful but suffocating valley. By way of flexing his moral muscles, he went to work training a horse for her, a dandy little mare out of a *manada* of sixteen he had captured after the Shevlin incident. She had intelligent ears and a tractable disposition. He wasted a week gentling her. It was his talent to be able to talk almost any horse out of so much as a crow-hop if he took time to explain things. The first time he mounted the mare, he rode her. She would make a nice, showy, going-away present. He pictured himself riding off down the valley, swinging his rope and driving his mustangs, while Susan, perhaps, shed a few tears. . . .

One day, after hobbling the bronchos by tying tails to front hoofs, they trailed back down to the ranch. He would let his catch gather here before ordering a boxcar and moving them along to the railroad. They turned all the horses into the trap except the mare, which he saddled and left rein-tied in the yard.

Susan came hurrying out, an apron snugly about her waist and flour to her elbows and in her hair. "I heard you on the trail and started a pie!" she told him. Then she saw the mare. "Whose is that?"

Wild-Horse felt as if he were enveloped in pink steam. Where pretty girls were concerned, it was always more blessed to give than to receive, and something about this girl brought him to his knees.

"She was too good for the cannery," he said. "She's yours."

Susan regarded the horse with gentle wonder. "She's the most beautiful. . . . What's her name?"

"Sister."

Susan threw off her apron and rode down to the water gap. They were two of a kind, she and the mare, dainty and spirited, but well-schooled in the proprieties. She came back to Wild-Horse, shining and tousled from the wind. "That's the nicest thing anybody ever did for me." Tears came to her eyes then. "Wild-Horse, I'm going to kiss you."

A species of terror assailed him. He backed off a step. All his fears of the valley rushed upon him. He had not turned the quicksand to stone, after all, but had been sucked deeper without realizing it. The mountains were rushing forward to bury him; the trees would march over the spot where lay the most colorful wild-horse trapper the West had ever known.

She halted, petulant but puzzled. "I was going to kiss you, not brand you."

The branding would come later.

"I . . . I haven't shaved," Wild-Horse fumbled.

"You're too thoughtful," Susan said. Without another word, she went back to the cabin.

At dinner she kept studying him. Women, thought Wild-Horse indignantly, were mighty contrary. If he'd tried to kiss *her,* he'd have been a brute. But when he hadn't let her kiss *him,* he was unnatural and mean—still a brute. He'd kissed girls aplenty, but this was one kiss he could not afford. He was right on the point of loving this girl as he had never loved even himself.

Suddenly she said: "Did you have any trouble up there? Old Moss has finally started suit for that land."

"I pasted Shevlin for nearly creasing me."

"Well, that did it! I've got to go and hire a lawyer, now."

Wild-Horse scowled at his plate. "Looks like all I've brought you is bad luck. Looks like I'd better move on to Whitten's."

"No, you don't! You contracted to clean out the broomtails, and you'll stay at it, mustanger."

Wild-Horse smothered a sigh. "Say," he said abruptly. "You haven't had any cattle stole lately, have you?"

"You mean by Moss? No, I wish I had. I'd send a sheriff up there in a hurry."

"Well, he's moonshining or something. Jittery as a coop full of catbirds."

He finished his half of the pie, arose, and said: "That was tolerable pie, miss." It was the best pie he had ever eaten, but he wasn't going to tell *her* so. Standing there in his awkwardness and uncertainty, he looked enormous, the kind of man you couldn't grow in a city, even as you couldn't grow a tree in a flower pot.

Noah Eagleson stared at him in bald admiration. "I'll bet you weighed a hundred and forty when you were born, Wild-Horse!"

"I was the runt of the litter," said Wild-Horse proudly. "I weighed four and a quarter pounds. I never caught up till I was fourteen. I had five brothers. They used to toss me back and forth like a rag doll. I had to step to keep up in that crowd, I can tell you! Then I began to grow. Didn't stop till I was twenty-four. I'm six foot three and an eighth in my bare feet . . . begging your pardon, miss."

Susan was gazing at him in a curious way, a light rising in her eyes, like a lamp flame warming and growing. "I might have guessed. . . ."

"How's that?" Wild-Horse asked.

"Nothing," she said. But she acted as if something very important had transpired. From that moment, she would beam at him whenever he would meet her eyes. She forced three more cups of coffee on him. He was bewildered.

Wild-Horse went back to the peaks determined to finish the work and get out. The girl and her valley were closing in on him.

Through the next two weeks, while summer ripened fully, the air filling with the smell of pine pitch and the ground burning with a brilliance of Alpine flowers, Wild-Horse Farnum's worries picked at him like a pawnbroker's fingers. The heart said—*Stay.*—common sense said—*Go.* Intuition, or vanity, said: *She loves you.* Wild-Horse was past denying that he loved her. But would they still love when the silk shirts wore out and the name Wild-Horse

Farnum rang like an aluminum half dollar? You could not expect a woman to go on praising and bending to a man after the honeymoon was over. Susan Brink would find herself married to a one-man rodeo, forever competing for points. It would be wonderful for about a month, and then it would be intolerable.

Most of the horses still seemed to run close to C. Y. Moss's range, so that he was hampered somewhat on his broncho chases. He thought sourly of this scrounging, uncourageous man with his worn-out overalls and expensive cigars. There was a reason why Moss wanted Susan Brink's mountain range. Wild-Horse was about persuaded to ride over and snoop around, when one day he saw smoke in the hills, and this gave him the push he had needed.

The smoke was a gray feather rising from a cañon. In about an hour he heard a restless movement of a small herd of cattle. He rode on until he saw a pole barrier across the head of the cañon and a lot of Hereford faces looking at him. But the men at the fire in the corral, C. Y. Moss and Elmo Shevlin, had not seen him yet. They were working fast, and Moss was talking a blue streak.

"No! Not so hard, Elmo! Burn that sack through and you might as well be using a running iron."

The steer lay on its side near the little branding fire. Moss held a wet gunnysack over an old brand while the ramrod thrust a branding iron against it.

"How many more?" Shevlin asked.

"About twenty."

Wild-Horse dropped a loop over a corral post and backed the horse until a section of the fence fell. The cattle streamed through. Tally book in hand, he sat there recording all the brands he could read. His carbine was across his lap.

He called to C. Y. Moss: "Was that over-bit red a Dollar Sign or a Panther Scratch?"

Moss blurted: "They aren't stolen! If they are, I didn't know it."

"He's a range dick!" declared Shevlin.

"It wouldn't have taken me a month to figure this out if I had been. I knew you were hiding a herd over by the railroad that day, but I thought it was going out, instead of coming in. I guess it's kind of ethical, at that. Never rustle around home when you can do it somewhere else and bring them in by rail. Let the brands heal and then ship them out again, hey?" He tossed the tally book to Moss. "Sign it. And let's not have any more talk about lawyers."

A wheedling look came into the rancher's eyes. "You want to trap over here, Farnum? I can show you where. . . ."

"All through trapping. At least, I've got my herd spotted. I won't run it in, though, until I have to."

It was almost too dramatic, he thought. The fearless mustanger saving the girl and riding into the sunset! It gave him goose-flesh. But there was no satisfaction in it, only sadness. It was a wonderful fade-out, but the picture would never completely fade. It would linger, tantalizing him with the vision of what he could not have, blurring his enjoyment of things he did have. Every time he put on a bucking show, he would think: *This is foolishness.*

Gloomily he rode back to the ranch as soon as they had taken another herd.

He was half-starved for the sight of her as he arrived at the Fiddleback for the last time. She came into the doorway and waved. Then she hurried toward him. The glow of the wood stove was in her face. She wore the white shirtwaist with the red ribbon she had worn in Council City. Her hair was braided and arranged in a kind of coronet across her head, and she had taken time to remove the apron. She began brightly: "I happened to hear you on the trail. . . ."

"And started a cake," Wild-Horse interrupted gloomily.

She bounced back. "It's not every woman who can bake at high altitudes, you know."

He turned away to tend the stock. He tried to look up at the mountains in a sneering way, the way they looked at him. But for the first time they were smiling. They glittered with evening sun imprisoned in snow and ice. *Time's running out!* Wild-Horse thought in panic. He made up his mind to leave right after dinner.

At the table, Susan was still full of chatter. "Wild-Horse, that little mare is perfect! I've ridden her every day. You certainly know how to break horses."

He tried to shrug it off, but was pleased, nonetheless.

"I hope you'll still be here for the rodeo in September. I'd love to see you ride again."

Noah grinned. "This here's a real mustanger, Sue . . . a ring-tailed roarer!"

Wild-Horse heard her saying gently: "No. This is a little boy starved for love and attention." Her face was full of warm tenderness. Desperately he ran for safety.

"I caught ol' Moss at it," he blurted. "He was slow-branding a herd of stolen cows they'd brought down by railroad and moved into the hills. Some of the brands are in this tally book. Use it if he ever gets butt-headed." He got up. "I'll eat that cake as I ride. I'm all finished with your range now."

He walked out. As he was saddling, she came to stand before him, gripping the edges of his vest. "Are you all finished with me, too, Wild-Horse?"

He had her shoulders in the pockets of his hands,

squeezing them hard and saying desperately: "I'll never be through with you, Sue! But if I stayed, you'd be through with me soon enough!"

"Why?"

"Because I'm a natural-born clown, a *prima donna* . . . whatever you want to call it. I like people to like me. I'd starve without applause. I guess I'm kind of a ham actor in chaps. Of course, there's the mountains, too. I'd die without them. But I'd fret myself to death up here."

"I know. I've been fretting myself to death here ever since Pop moved to the Pioneers' Home."

He hesitated. "What have you got to fret about?"

"I'm as bad off in my way as you are in yours. You said you were the youngest of six children. Wild-Horse, I was the *eldest* of five! When Mom died, I had all those kids to bring up. I had four noses to wipe and four pairs of jeans and dresses to wash, not counting my own. I thought it was monotonous, until they all married or moved away, and just me and Pop were left. I felt like a widow, or something. And then Pop left. And when I saw you acting up with your horse that day, I thought . . . here's somebody that needs me! Here's a boy that doesn't have anybody to darn his socks and comb his hair. The lonesome ones always act this way."

Common sense rallied for the last time. "But you'll get tired of it! You'll have . . . other things to mother after a while."

"But by that time I'll have you weaned. I weaned all the others and set them on their feet, didn't I? And on top of that, I happen to love you." She let her hands drop away and was suddenly soft and pliant. "Well, I had to tell you. Everything looked right, to me, but if it doesn't to you. . . ."

She went back into the house. Wild-Horse slowly took

the latigo in his hands, and started to tighten the cinch. He faltered. He then climbed the corral, and rolled a cigarette. He smoked four, and climbed down. He dropped the last cigarette, took off the saddle, and turned the horse into the trap.

When he entered the kitchen, Noah and Sue were eating cake. A third piece, creamy-white and with chocolate icing as thick as a boot sole, was at his place. He ate it, drank his coffee, and leaned back. "Did I ever show you this one?" he asked.

He made a half dollar crawl across his knuckles and disappear into his palm.

Noah cackled. "Did you ever see the like of him?" he asked Susan.

She laughed, with tears in her eyes. "No," she said. "I never did."

River Man

Davey Leathers turned from the glowing furnace door, ash hoe in his hands, as Sid Logan, first mate aboard the Missouri River packet, *Sherrod*, came down off the boiler deck. Logan was a heavy-shouldered, bull-necked man with a hard, square jaw and angry black eyes.

He stared at Davey, the flames reddening his blunt features. Then his glance snapped to big, grizzled Tom Stinger, chief engineer.

"Are you deaf, Stinger?" he barked. "Ain't you heard the pilot ringing for steam the last half hour?"

Davey watched Tom Stinger with a bright gleam in his eyes. Old Tom left off tinkering with the doctor, the steam pump that kept his boilers full, and faced Logan. He was four inches over six feet and built like a bull buffalo. His seamy face, with its stand of gray whiskers that never seemed to get more than a quarter of an inch long, was full of derision.

"That brass pounder's been hangin' on the bell ever since we left Fort Benton," he drawled. "If you'll notice, the clapper o' the bell is now tied down permanent. If Mister Murdo don't like the way I build my fires, he can climb down and build his own."

Sid Logan's jowls purpled as he glared at the Irishman, but he only grunted and walked past him to where Davey stood. He yanked the hoe from his grasp, and grubbed around in the red coals, then he shoved the handle back at the eighteen-year-old engineer's cub.

"If you'd keep the ashes down," Logan said, "you'd keep your b'lers hot. Clean that box out, now, and heave a rick o' wood into 'er."

Davey gave him a stolid stare. "Forty mile to the next wood station, and us short," he said. "Guerrillas burnt all the wood back at Wolf Point. Plumb bad if we run out and have to drift. . . ."

"Maybe"—Logan scowled—"you'd like to come up and show the pilot how to run his boat."

He stalked off, but at the runway turned back. Davey watched his face, noting the sweat that crawled down from his thick, curly, black hair. Sid Logan had been more overbearing than ever since they had left Fort Benton two days ago. But, oddly, there was a look of terror on him now.

In a low, husky tone he said: "Maybe you've forgot what kind of a cargo we're freightin'. There's a half million in gold in the captain's safe! Don't think Jeff Davis's guerrillas are going to let us lay on this river all summer. They boarded the *Miss Hannah* last month while she was takin' on wood. Shot down the crew and the free blacks she was takin' to the Dakotas."

Logan's eyes flinched as they roamed along the near bank, questing among the matted wild rose bushes and willows. "Maybeso them bushes is crawlin' with guerrillas right now," he breathed. "Hopin' to put a ball through the pilot's head and wreck the ship. Them soldiers we're carryin' won't help us none, then. We're freightin' something the Union needs more'n blacks. Gold to buy guns with! Gold to pay soldiers with! Do you savvy, Stinger, we've got to have steam to get through!"

Stinger said harshly, his eyes fuming under shaggy gray brows: "It'll take more'n a groanin' steam drum to get this tub to Council Bluffs. You can tell Murdo that for me. Tell 'im he'll get his steam, if he savvies to use it."

Sid Logan's back stiffened, his mouth twitching. "One of these fine days," he said slowly, "you're going to find you ain't even fit to rake ashes on a first-class steamboat. Hang this up where you'll remember it. There's no place for a coward on the Big Muddy. Sometime that yellow streak of yours is going to crop out again. And when it does . . . you're done!"

Davey Leathers would have sprung after him, but for the paw that clamped on his shoulder. "Easy, pup," Tom Stinger said.

The boy stood trembling under his grasp, his eyes blazing. Davey was almost as tall as the mate, but it was a ragged, spindle-shanked five foot ten that was his. He would never be heavy. He was of lean, slab-sided make, his body hard as boiler-plate. His features were thin, eyes dark with an ever-present hankering. His scrubby blond hair hadn't been cut in four months.

"Damn him!" he choked. "Damn four-flushin' wharf scum. Raisin' his voice to the best pilot that ever swung a wheel from here to N'Orleans!"

"That was yesterday," Tom Stinger said gently. "Someday, pup, we'll show 'em again. We're on now. Git to your in-jine."

Muttering, the boy went off through the hodge-podge of reeking black machinery to relieve the second engineer's striker at the larboard engine. Tom would be taking over starboard. The very notion of it—Tom Stinger, standing like a run-of-the-mill engineer among his cams and gauges—was gall. *Mister* Tom Stinger, whose name had once been breathed with those of Horace Bixby and Sam Clemens when river men talked of lightning pilots! The same Tom Stinger who had taken the *A. L. Shotwell* from

New Orleans to Cairo for a standing record.

Davey nourished the conviction that someday Tom would again stand with his great varnished wheel before him. As he had stood those first two years Davey had known him, when he was his cub. But he was coming to know more thoroughly the contempt in which river men held those who lost their nerve. Tom Stinger had left his reputation and his courage in the old *Lizzie Barton*, when she blew a steam drum in Bayou Lafitte.

Ancient boiler-plate was the culprit. Other pilots, jealous of him, bandied it about that he had been crowding on too much steam to beat another ship. Thirty passengers had been scalded to death or drowned in the disaster. The story was started that Tom Stinger had lost his nerve after the tragedy. That he sweated buckets every hitch. That he was done. And that was all that was needed, on the river, to finish a man.

Tom and Davey Leathers ended up, one day, in the engine room of a packet plying between St. Louis and Fort Benton on the Big Muddy. But always old Tom's heart was up in the wheelhouse, with the clean breeze against his face and the spokes under his hands.

The hours of Davey's hitch went slowly. It was dusk when the second engineer's cub came to relieve him. Davey found Tom Stinger in the engine room. Murdo, who had just come off duty, was with him.

Murdo was a long drink of a man with a sour face and a drawling affectation of speech. Like many top-notch wheelmen, he dressed fit to kill. His boots were high-heeled and shiny, with tassels, and his britches fitted like wet chamois. He greased his hair until it glistened, and twisted his mustache ends into sword points.

Murdo inspected the weights Tom had flung on the escape valve arm for extra steam. Then, with his soft fingers, he gestured at the furnace. "Are you trying to freeze something in here?" he demanded. "There isn't enough steam in this tub to operate a tin whistle. What's the matter with your resin?"

Said Tom Stinger: "Not a thing. I'm savin' that resin for whenever we need some damn' hot fires in a hurry. You ain't forgot Tobacco Island?"

Murdo's lazy eyes opened a little wider, as if he hadn't thought as far ahead as Tobacco Island. Then he shrugged. "I thought someone would have the good sense to bring along an adequate supply of fuel. . . ."

Tom winked at Davey as the pilot stalked to the forecastle stairs. "He knows damn' well we got the last two bar'ls o' resin in Fort Benton."

They went forward and stood among barrels and boxes at the bow. The water, whitish in the deepening dusk, stretched ahead of them as still as a pond. At moments like this, between sleep and the long hours in the engine room, Tom Stinger seemed almost happy. He would fill Davey with the lore of the river man, set his brain afire with the thrill of piloting a ship. He would test his memory of the things he had told him time and again.

"Yonder whirlpool." He pointed with the chewed stem of his corncob pipe. "What do you make of it?"

Davey went tense with scanning the almost invisible swirl of currents. "Reef bein' washed away. She'll be like to form forty, fifty foot lower down."

"Cuss you, pup!" Tom roared. "That spot's goin' to be too shoal to pass next trip! That's the mark o' shoalin' water. Learn that! Or someday you'll pile your ship so high dry ladders can't reach 'er! Yonder streak, now . . . ?"

78

Davey bit his lip, his gaze beating into the dark. There was a hurting in his throat. Tom's rebuke was a fearful thing for him. In the daytime he would have answered before the question was fully put. But a pilot must know his river four ways—upstream, downstream, night, and day.

"That there's a . . . a snag."

Tom Stinger gave out with a boatman's curse, lurid and stinging. "Wind reef!" he barked. "If you skirt every one o' them, you'll pilot the slowest tub on the Big Muddy."

Then his snapping blue eyes softened, and he nudged the miserable cub. "Tell you something, pup. Mister Murdo's cub, up yonder in the pilot house, is makin' the same mistakes. This ol' river's lower'n I've ever seed 'er. He's been a-dodgin' the marks the wind makes and runnin' full onto sawyers. Murdo ain't a passel better. He's a-countin' on higher water after we pass the Yellowstone. But, mark you, she'll be worse!"

The next morning, when they passed the mouth of the Yellowstone and saw the muddy trickle crawling from it, old Tom's prediction was borne out. Murdo went up to the wheelhouse with a deep furrow between his eyes. It was four hours later, when Tom and Davey were taking their off hitch up on the hurricane deck before the pilothouse that Murdo's lanky, freckled cub, Peters, came and made talk with them.

"That ol' Muddy's shore low," he offered. "I reckon nobody ever took a ship through shoaler water'n this."

"She ain't been took through, yet." Tom Stinger continued to smoke and read the face of the river. There was a quiet broken by the voices of soldiers on the boiler deck, by the jingle of bells in the heart of the ship, by the muted threshing of the paddles.

A turn in the river suddenly threw them squarely upon the wreck of the old *Sioux City*. For ten years the splintered hulk had laid there for pilots to take warning by, or to pile into in the night.

Stinger frowned. Last trip there had been ample water to each side of her. But now it was a question of which channel to try.

On the larboard, the *Sherrod* would crowd the willow and chokecherry tangle of the mainland bank. Guerrilla guns might lurk in those thickets. To starboard, there were shoals and a snag.

Peters's voice came heavy with exaggerated nonchalance. "Mister Murdo reckoned he'd take her through to larboard. What you think now?"

Stinger spat overside, winked at Davey. "You tell Mister Murdo, if he wants my advice, he can come and ask for it personal."

Peters jumped back. His freckled face twisted. "Mister Murdo don't need the advice of a has-been pilot no time! I reckon he c'd give you plenty . . . about keepin' your steam drum in one piece."

Above them, Murdo's voice roared for Peters. Down below, bells were jangling as he rang for half speed larboard and full speed starboard. The *Sherrod* began to warp closer to the wreck, making for the channel between it and the mainland. Peters ran for the pilothouse. Davey's fury-filled eyes followed him.

Lines folded into the skin about Stinger's eyes. His lips tautened. "Look you, pup," he said, his voice husky. "Mark that wake to sta'board o' the *Sioux City*. That's a planter. Said stump is a scant quarter under the surface. We could clear her, but not the shoals. She'll draw one less quarter in the channel, judgin' by the marks on the bank."

"Too shoal," Davey grunted.

"Not if a man savvies his boat. I'd bear down full steam, ring for full steam astern just as she took the bar. That throws her high in the front, and she clears her bow. Then full speed ag'in, and over we go, with a scrapin' and a groanin' like you never heard. But we're over."

"Mister Murdo," Davey pointed out breathlessly, "don't see it that way. He's takin' us through on the other side."

"Pray the Lord there ain't guerrillas on the bank," the engineer said. "Hunker down by the chimney, whilst we go through."

The *Sherrod*, her gleaming white Texas and tall iron chimneys towering above the matted brush of the bosque, nosed into the narrow channel formed by derelict and bank. Old Tom Stinger hunkered in a half crouch, deep-set eyes studying the river. To larboard, overhanging branches almost brushed the gingerbread railings of boiler and main decks. The *Sioux City*, stark and faded, loomed at the other side to rake the packet should she drift too close.

Then his thoughts exploded, as from the bank a salvo of shots poured into the wheelhouse.

Broken glass rained down on them where they squatted. There was a sharp cry from Murdo, and a body struck the floor. Again the leaves of the willows stirred. Balled lead hammered into the pilothouse. A moment later the *Sherrod* rammed heavily against the bank.

Lead and flame lashed back across the narrow strip of water, as the soldiers fired blindly into the ambuscade of the guerrillas. Davey lay on his belly, fingers digging at the planks, flesh crawling as he awaited a bullet. Tom Stinger's hand gripped his shoulder.

Now the wheelhouse door flew open, and Captain

Gallatin stood in the aperture. It was an astounding thing the slight, red-faced man called down. "Stinger! Stinger, get up here! Murdo and Peters are both down! I can't run this thing!"

Now! Davey thought. *Now they'll savvy whether Tom Stinger is a coward.* The thought was hardly formed when Tom's hand was dragging him to his feet and he was being hauled to the ladder.

"Up you go, pup!" Tom commanded. Davey scuttled up the ladder like a monkey. A bullet tore into a rung, cutting his hand with splinters. Then he was inside the pilot-house.

Murdo lay before the wheel, a bullet through his head. Peters, his breast torn with a dozen balls, was huddled near him, gasping out his life in strangling breaths. Slivers of glass sprinkled the carpet. The varnished walls were torn with bullets. One of the wheel spokes was shot away and a ragged stump remained.

Sid Logan stood beside Captain Gallatin. Logan's dry tongue kept fumbling over his lips. For once there was no sarcasm on his face.

"Get us off that bank!" he roared. "Another minute and they'll board us."

"They ain't enough to board us," said Stinger. "But they'll damn' soon have us afire."

Captain and mate whirled to look aft. Davey's glance went with theirs. He saw the blazing raft the guerrillas had shoved into the channel. It was perhaps a hundred yards astern and bearing down so that it would come to rest under their landing stages.

In Tom Stinger's eyes there was a hard, eager shine. He stood with both gnarled hands on the wheel, his gaze whipping downward through the shattered windows. There was nothing cowardly about the way he stood up under the threat of those hidden guns. Now he yanked a bell cord.

Seconds later the big paddles began to thresh the water. The *Sherrod* grated off the bank. Stinger wheeled her so that her paddles would strike the raft before the landing stages could be set afire. They were back in mid-channel when, from the momentarily silent bosque, a single rifle roared.

At the pilot's side a hanging lamp shattered into a million diamonds. Coal oil burst into flame, ignited by a spark from the impact of the ball with the bracket. Tom Stinger staggered back.

He sank to his knees, pawing his face. Burning oil ran blue and yellow over his head and shoulders. With a cry Davey was on him, beating out the flames with a curtain he had yanked from a window. Tom did not get up immediately when the fire was out. Logan and Captain Gallatin were stamping out the flames that licked over the rug. But the eyes Tom lifted to Davey were dull.

"Take the wheel, pup! I . . . I ain't seein' no good."

"Tom . . . !"

"Take the wheel!" Tom Stinger roared.

Davey bounded to the wheel. Straddling Murdo's body, he clutched the spokes. His heart thumped like a fist against his ribs. All the lessons he had had from Tom were in his mind at once. Biting his lip, he sorted through them. The *Sherrod* was on the point of backing into the derelict now. He rang full speed ahead and waited with hands sweaty on the spokes.

A tremor ran through the packet. Slowly she stopped and, as her wheels reversed, slipped ahead. The raft was deluged by a cataract of tawny water.

Davey kept his attention riveted on the path of water before him. He closed his mind to the bullets that hammered into the flimsy wall, that rang off the iron chimneys like anvil strokes. The packet handled clumsily under his un-taught hands. A score of things must be kept in mind—the ripples and wakes on the river, the wheel, the drift, the proper signals.

Pain made Tom Stinger's voice raspy. "How's she lay?"

"Abreast o' the *Sioux City*. Clear water ahead."

"Then swing 'er! Put the Texas twixt us and them devils."

Davey felt the big ship turning under his feet. With the officers' cabin to shield them from the snipers, the attack from shore ceased. The *Sherrod* steamed on, with a blind man and a raw hand for pilots.

Through that endless afternoon, with the sun burning his cheek, Davey tooled the packet. Captain Gallatin bathed and treated Tom's eyes. Tom vowed it was like looking through a Louisiana fog with the plantations burning cane on the windward bank. With difficulty, he could make out the prow.

Nervousness rode Davey Leathers heavily. His eyes ached with ceaseless searching of the brown strip of water. Without Tom Stinger at his elbow they would have been wrecked before sundown. From the shore marks Davey described, Tom was able to tell him where lurked hidden snags and rocks. Once, when the distant barking of a dog came to their ears, Tom himself piled onto the wheel.

"Sandbar dead ahead! Watch for 'er! That hound allus welcomes us."

A moment later the *Sherrod* scraped by a reef the water had failed to tell of. It was such a memory as Tom's that made a pilot.

As night pulled a black curtain across the river, Davey

felt as if the ship were steaming into a weird half world. The Missouri lay a milky path beneath him. Everything was changed. No longer could he reckon the depth of the river by water marks on the banks. Wind reef and true reef were indistinguishable. It was at such times that the lightning pilot thumbed the pages of his incredible memory for aid. But when midnight brought them to Disaster Bend, even Tom Stinger shied.

"Shoalest stretch of water on the Big Muddy," he told the cub. "Put a leadsman on the bow."

With a deck hand perched on the bow, slinging his lead, they pushed gingerly into the bend. The leadsman's cries were an eerie sound in the dark.

"Half twain! Half twain! Quarter less twain! *Mark one!*"

Davey rang for reverse engines, his heart pounding. Down below, on the hurricane deck, a small, winking light had been distracting him for minutes. Now, for the first time, he was conscious of what it was.

"Cigar on the hurricane," he told Tom. "Looks like Sid Logan. Wait a minute . . . Tom." He held his voice down to a harsh whisper. "I'll eat that cigar if he ain't signalin' with it."

"You're woolgatherin'," Stinger told him. Groping his way to the window, he shouted at the smoker. "Douse that cigar, damn you!"

The cigar was hastily flung into the water. A few minutes later, the *Sherrod* successfully passed the shoals. But Davey Leathers was not sure that he had been woolgathering, nor that Tom thought he had been.

Dawn found him bleary-eyed, mentally and physically burned out. His lean face had picked up a fine webbing of wrinkles about the mouth and eyes. Pounds had evaporated from his spare frame. Not for a minute during the night had he let his attention wander. But daylight brought a tendency to let down.

Tom Stinger sensed that in the way Davey called off the landmarks. Suddenly his strong fingers were biting into the boy's shoulder.

"Lettin' up, eh? What kind of a lily-fingered weaklin' are you, that a little trick like you've done leaves you noddin'?"

"I've been on fourteen hours," Davey said defensively.

"Fourteen hours! I stood the wheel thirty-six durin' the flood of 'Forty-Four. Your time ain't come yet by a heap. Listen to me. You mind Tobacco Island. Remember how we skinned through on the way up? There'll be no such thing done this trip. We've got to go behind the island, where the water's deep."

"Tobacco Island!" The boy's eyes lost their dullness. "That's where they boarded the *Bayou Queen*! The red legs are thick in there. It'll be like turnin' the boat over to 'em."

Tom sat down again, rubbing his sore eyes. "She's got to be done. Mind the wheel."

Davey's body was in a bath of cold sweat. What had happened at the *Sioux City* would be nothing compared to Tobacco Island. From both sides, red legs could pour their lead into the ship. There were said to be hundreds of Confederate guerrillas in the vicinity, hard-riding, straight-shooting men who took for their badge leggings of red morocco leather. Davey thought of logs anchored in the channel behind the island, of rocks dumped where they would tear the bottom out of the ship.

Somehow, word was passed that an attack was expected at Tobacco Island. The soldiers, who had been rough-housing on the lower decks, fell into silence. The low singing of Negro roustabouts was stilled. All eyes were for the river. All were watching for the brush-clad island of horseshoe shape that was set in a small backwater of the same form. For two hundred yards the *Sherrod* must pass between crowding, overgrown banks.

In the middle of the morning, when Davey Leathers thought he could no longer hold his heavy lids open, a low shape like a pall of smoke materialized far down the Muddy. He described it, thick-tongued, to Tom. Tom pulled himself to his feet.

"Tobacco Island," he muttered. "Gimme the tube. We'll use that resin now."

Stinger held the speaking tube to his lips, bawling an order that echoed back to them from the engine room. The whole ship was waiting for that command. As blacker smoke began to spew from the chimneys, a heavier throb of engines could be felt, and officers came to stand silently in the pilothouse. There was Captain Gallatin nervously clicking his false teeth, and Major Shell, in charge of the troops, smoothing his heavy yellow mustaches with a gloved finger.

The second mate and some other officers formed a tight knot, muttering monotoned comments. Sid Logan loomed at Davey's left hand, chewing his blunt cigar.

Tom Stinger knew, and Davey knew, that these men were very humble, now, who not so long ago had had scorn for an aging pilot who had turned yellow. For they had seen him in as black an hour as a river man had ever known and had seen the mettle of him shine bright and clean. They were humble—and a little scared. Even a brave man can know fear in the moment before death strikes.

Davey Leathers bit his lip and wished that feeling of butterflies in his stomach would cease. He was plumb scared out of his wits, watching Tobacco Island resolve out of the haze into a low, tree-clad island. But he'd have died before he forsook his wheel. He told Tom breathlessly what he read as the channel's mouth opened to swallow them. The fog in Tom Stinger's eyes was clearing a little now, making him all the more impatient that he couldn't see enough to handle the wheel, but beyond the bow of the ship all was gray mist and blurred shadows to his vision. He heard Davey out, and grunted his recommendations.

The *Sherrod* crept nervously into the shady canal, with its irritating hordes of biting insects and its frilled banks. Safely into it, the water clear, Davey rang for full steam ahead. He wanted to sink down, to hide under something. Of all the targets the ship offered, he was the one they would take first. Stuck up there on the front of that frail, bullet-riddled shack on the hurricane deck, he was like a squirrel on top of a log—a cinch shot.

Sid Logan walked to the rear of the cabin, and Davey's lips tightened. Logan knew a dangerous spot when he was in one. They were halfway through the bayou-like corridor and nothing had happened. Rotting cottonwood leaves filled the cabin with a fetid stench. The screaming tension increased.

Then it exploded.

A swish of sound like that of a thrown rope was all the warning the *Sherrod* had. A moment later the ship came to a lurching, bulkhead-straining stop. Then it was as if both banks ran with fire. From each side Rebel lead slashed at them. A roar of musketry shook the leaves of the cottonwoods. Half the men in the wheelhouse would have been killed in the initial barrage, but for the fact that the sudden stop had hurled them all to the floor. Davey alone remained upright, hanging, terrified, to his wheel.

A glance below and he gasped: "Red legs! Boardin' us!"

The trees of the island were giving up their hordes of red leg guerrillas. Over the side they came, spilling onto the main deck. A wild nightmare band, shaggy, bewhiskered, clad in buckskins and tattered woolens, fearless and bloodthirsty as wolves. Men with nothing to lose, and plunder to win. By the dozen they were shot down, and sprawled back into the strip of water they had jumped.

Gallatin was at the window, emptying his Navy pistol into the squirming horde. Tom Stinger bellowed into Davey's ear.

"What'sa matter? Why don't she move?"

"They've throwed a line over our mooring bitt. We're fast!"

Tom cursed.

Davey yelled: "Shall I back her and try it again?"

"You'll only tear her guts out. That line's got to be cut. You, down there!" Tom leaned out of the window, unmindful of shots. "Cut that line!"

But in the bedlam no one heard him. The guerrillas on the mainland were trying to cover for the boarding party by sending salvo after salvo into the ship. The soldiers aboard were outnumbered three to one. Major Shell sprang down the ladder to join his men, Gallatin and the rest following him.

Tom Stinger fumbled his old six-shooter from his belt. "Take it," he told Davey. "Shoot hell out of that line. Then full steam ahead and maybe we can bust 'er."

Davey whirled to the window. Bracing the barrel of the revolver over the sill, he squinted. A hard ring of coldness pressed against his spine, bunching his nerves into knots.

Sid Logan said: "When that 'un goes off, mister, so does this 'un. Drop it."

The ice melted from Davey's brain. Fury and a vast

contempt twisted through him. "Still think I was woolgatherin', Tom? This loud-mouthed river cull *was* signalin' with that cigar! It was him that passed the word we were comin'."

Logan's finger visibly tensed on the trigger. It was not patience that held the bullet, but a lack of courage to murder in cold blood. His lips stretched tightly.

"If you don't drop that gun. . . ."

Tom Stinger said hurriedly: "Drop it, Davey. He's gonna shoot."

Davey let the gun fall. At full cock, it went off when it struck, sending a ball between Davey and the mate, through the ceiling. The roar caused Sid Logan to start. In the next instant big Tom Stinger was on him.

Stinger drove him against the wheel, his hairy fist smashing into Logan's face. Logan fought like a tiger, not making a sound, but his gun went off twice. The second shot took a tiny chunk out of Tom's ear.

Quickly Davey bent and retrieved the smoking .45. Gripping the gun by the barrel, he came up fast behind Sid Logan. The gun chopped twice. Blood and hair came away on the butt plates the second time.

With his foot, Tom Stinger rolled the traitor out of the way. "As I was sayin'," he growled, "a few shots might cut that hawser to where we could break it."

"Aye, aye, sir," Davey said.

He emptied both guns into the hawser, watching the heavy hempen line jump at each shot. But it still seemed as stout as ever when he reached for the bell pull and rang half speed astern.

A score of red legs were dumped into the river as the *Sherrod* pulled away. Fifty feet above, Davey grabbed up the speaking tube. "All you've got. Full steam ahead!"

The packet hit the end of the line with a shock that seemed to rip her apart. One of the glowing chimneys tore from its moorings and crashed into the river in a geyser of steam. The line held. Then Davey saw the mooring bitt tilt. It tore loose, taking out a piece of deck ten feet square as it was yanked out by the bolts.

Shuddering, the packet began to stir forward. Shouting red legs sprang into the water, trying to reach the landing stages. Davey could feel each thud as the big paddles sucked them under and broke them like twigs. He was conscious of bullets singing about him. But suddenly there was the wine of victory in his blood, intoxicating him. He could see daylight ahead. With a surge of bravado, he pulled the whistle cord and blasted a river man's good bye. They were clear.

For a mile, the boat shed red legs like barnacles. Dog-eared, dilapidated, she rolled on downriver. Davey Leathers was moved to sing a keelboat man's song as they plowed on toward Council Bluffs.

At midnight, the *Sherrod* limped up to the dock at Council Bluffs. Fifteen dead men were carried off before the Union's gold was touched. Sid Logan was among them.

Up in the pilothouse, Captain Gallatin shook Tom Stinger's hand warmly. "I don't know who merits the credit, Stinger, you or the boy. The river's never seen a finer piece of piloting. There's a place for you two on this ship as long as you want it."

Tom Stinger's eyes sparkled. He winked at Davey. "Pilot this old tub? I guess not. Come, Davey, my lad. Yonder's Mister Jory, pilot of the *Natchez*, come to swap windies with us. Doubtless tomorrow we'll do him the honor of shippin' as far as Saint Louis with him in the wheelhouse. But first . . . a beer in the Frontier Bar."

A beer in the Frontier Bar—with Tom Stinger, while an admiring river crowd watched! Davey's walk took on a proud swagger as he and Tom went down to the landing stage. For Tom Stinger was a name to breathe respectfully on this man's river, and any cub of his was a man in his own right.

Payment Past Due

Sullivan had heard an axiom in this country that a good stage team could always outrun a saddle horse. Up there on the box, the driver was trying to prove it. He was leaning out over the clattering void between the dashboard and the horses' rumps with the ribbons clutched in one lanky, gauntleted fist, shouting at them and letting the buckskin popper sting. Catclaw and mesquite, wet with recent rain, slashed at the muddy panels of the coach as it boomed across sandy arroyos and up over brushy ridges in the wide, mountain-hemmed valley. Now and then the floorboard came down on the reach-and-bolsters with a jar that shook the frightened passengers like pullets in a sack.

On the deck, Sullivan heard the voice of section boss Ed Blocker bawling imprecations at no one in particular as he fired at the horsemen streaming along the road behind them. Sullivan pressed to the window, trying to peer back, but seldom getting a look because of the brush screening the turns. McFall, the Tucson man who had been trying to convince Sam Sullivan that Arizona was really a pretty quiet place, got in a shot, and the wind whipped the sound and smoke away. McFall was a bald, florid man with a black mustache straddling his mouth like an oxbow and swinging up to join his sideburns. He shoved the still-smoking Colt at the girl who sat between them.

"Load!" He had another gun that he shifted to his right hand.

Sullivan was a little surprised at himself. He had been so

sunken in doubtful self-examination these last months that it surprised him whenever he did something requiring courage. Even when the stage had first been stopped, when the outlaws had been leveling saddle guns at the windows of the coach, he had been wondering whether it would pay to try to reach his Navy pistol as he made to climb out. There was nothing much they could take from him but a small amount of money, a watch, and some surgical instruments, but he had feared for McFall's daughter, who was the most attractive loot in the coach. Then the driver had suddenly let his whip fly and half tore the sack mask from the head of the man who sat his horse in the middle of the road. In that same shocked instant, he had kicked off the brake, given the horses the whip, and let the coach thunder across the arroyo.

Now the coach swerved into a turn. Over the blurred gray-green tangle of brush, Sullivan saw the riders behind. Their ponies were blowing hard and strings of froth pulled from the bits. Letting the long-barreled Colt line out on them, he fired. He saw one man clutch at the horn of his saddle. Again the Concord hit a pothole, and, when Sullivan picked himself up off the floor, he heard Blocker, the section boss, bawling: "They've quit, by God! We dropped one!"

McFall sank back. He reached over to shake Sullivan's hand. "File a notch on that gun of yours," he said, "and call me a liar. But it's the first of such doin's I've seen in a year. Somebody must have known Ed Blocker would be bringing the box up."

Katie, his daughter, handed back his extra gun, half loaded, and seemed to melt against the seat. Sullivan had ammonium salts in the bag at his feet. For an instant he thought she was going to need them. But after a moment she opened her eyes. "That seems to spoil our story, doesn't it? If it weren't for Will Spence, up there, you'd be sitting by the road with your pockets hanging out now."

Sullivan laughed. She smiled, seeming reassured, and he liked the way her cheeks tinged with color. Good, healthy color. He liked her eyes, too, the cool, violet-gray of a smoke tree. Her hair was brown, brushed and parted and worn low on her neck.

At Cienega Creek station, they turned out for a stretch while teams were changed. Sullivan had coffee with the rest in the mean, mud-and-pole station. He made an entry in the journal he kept. The hold-up would be something to write home about. He set it down briefly, including his feeling that he had met one of the outlaws previously. The voice had been familiar. Then his eyes went back to the entry he had scrawled that morning while they had watered the horses at a small stream.

Met two freight wagons owned by wheat buyer named Martin, who brings *panocha* from Mexico to mill in Tucson. A pleasant, well-dressed man, for a bullwhacker. Wore the sharp-toed Mexican boots many of them wear. Yellow as butter.

He had a cool jolt of surprise. The voices *had* been alike, and by heaven the boots had been identical! But how could a man in a bull wagon travel faster than a stagecoach? For they had passed Martin's train three hours before the attack. While he was mulling this over, Ed Blocker, who was returning from El Paso with the company strongbox, tromped in, seeking Tom McFall. Blocker was a big, hearty man in a buckskin shirt and old cavalry pants. He wore a beaded Indian belt and a single cedar-handled Colt on his left hip, butt foremost. He had Spence, the driver, in tow.

"Tom, will you have a look at this galoot?"

Spence, a lean, stringy man with a face weathered like a finger post, shrugged it off. "One of them grooved me is all. She don't stop bleedin'." He was holding his forearm. His sleeve was soaked and his hand shone darkly red.

"Let's see it," McFall said importantly.

Sullivan watched McFall's thumb probe for a blood vessel that was not there. Blood continued to flow in a steady, strong stream from the deep rut across the driver's arm. The man's face was already ashen. McFall, sweating, chewed his lip. "Dangedest thing *I* ever saw," he muttered.

Sullivan hesitated, wary of saying more than he had to. "I didn't know you were a doctor," he remarked.

"Me? Hell, I'm only a druggist, but I'm the nearest thing to a doctor Tucson's got."

"Is that right? I'm a drug salesman. I've seen a lot of surgeons work. Now, it seems to me. . . ."

McFall slid along the bench. "Take over!"

Sullivan's hands went to work. It was odd, watching them, as though they were someone else's hands, not the hands they used to praise in medical school, the hands that had turned against him the year he had started to practice. The blood ceased to flow as if a faucet had been turned off. He rigged a tourniquet, and stood up.

"For a drug salesman," McFall exclaimed, "you work like a regular city sawbones!"

Ed Blocker regarded him curiously.

"I'll ride with you the rest of the way," Sullivan told Spence. "That will have to be loosened once in a while." He went outside. He knew they were puzzled, but he was damned if he would relieve their curiosity. He was only sorry his ticket included a stopover in Tucson. Somewhere out West, he had thought, he would make a new start, hang out his shingle as though no shadow were over it. But in those few moments in the station, some of the old uncertainty had returned, just an edge of it showing, but enough to remind him that you could not leave shadows behind. They had a way of following.

Dusk sprawled across the desert as they entered Tucson. The pueblo lay in a wedge of puckered hills, a river touching the town on the west, near the old wall. A belt of farms showed where water had been carried in ditches. The pueblo itself was a drab core; it was a town of church bells, crows, and rubbish. It had the appearance of a thriving town, but it was a rough one, dirty, and careless of its appearance, like a bleary-eyed old man with food spilled on his vest.

He stood with the McFalls at the rear of the stage as luggage was unloaded. Lamps were being set in the sockets of the Concord. "This is a growin' place, Mister Sullivan," McFall bragged. "You ought to think about making it your permanent home."

"The company's sending me to San Francisco. I'm just stopping over to break the trip."

He was gratified that Katie McFall looked disappointed. "If you know any young doctors in the East, tell them about us. We haven't had a doctor since the Army moved out five years ago. There are enough patients for at least three good doctors."

The station agent brought his heavy cowhide bag. "Here you are, Doctor."

The McFalls stared at him.

Sullivan smiled. "You've been talking to the driver."

"No. They've got you down as Samuel A. Sullivan,

M.D., on the waybill," the agent said. "There's only one Sullivan. You *are* Doctor Sullivan, aren't you?"

Sullivan accepted the bag. "That's right. What's the best hotel?"

McFall slapped him on the back. "A joker, eh? By grabs, I said to Katie . . . 'Nobody that hadn't studied medicine ever handled a wound thataway!' What are you trying to put over on us?"

He was taken charge of by the McFalls, who appeared to regard a doctor with veneration, awe, and excitement. Sullivan had to make some sort of explanation. "You see, so many of these desert towns have no doctor that they all but kidnap you."

"I should have thought"—Katie frowned—"you'd have stayed on at the first town you found where they didn't have a doctor."

"Say." McFall was staring at his daughter. "There's no reason he needs to stay in that flea-bag of a hotel and get bit by every sort of vermin in Arizona. There's that little office on Market that ain't being used. There's a cot in it. We can fix him up with blankets and. . . ."

It was useless to protest. In an hour's time, Katie had swept the place out, McFall had brought fresh water and clean blankets and laid a fire on the corner hearth. Sullivan smiled wearily. He was a lanky, dark-haired man who needed weight on his bones. His mouth had a sardonically humorous turn.

"This begins to look like coercion," he remarked.

Katie laughed, her eyes still picking critically at the room. "We're going to let your conscience be your guide. After you see some of these poor, unhappy people of ours, you won't be able to leave."

Sullivan shook his head. "I'm sorry. I took the layover in

order to rest. If it gets out that I'm taking patients, I'll leave here in worse condition than I am now. They'll have me up all night and riding twenty miles out of town to treat patients."

The girl's eyes did not comprehend. Her lips tightened as she looked at him. She said slowly: "I don't know how you can be so cold. Are sick people any different here than in the East?"

"Katie!" Her father spoke sharply. He shook hands with Sullivan with no trace of rancor. "Like she says, we'll let your conscience be your guide. You've got four days till the next stage. Think it over, Doctor."

It was the look on the girl's face that bothered him. Disapproving. Puzzled. Disdain making a pinch between her eyes. *Damn it,* he thought, *what does she know about me?* She'd turn him loose on her poor, unhappy people and one or two of them might be a whole lot more unhappy when he finished. A man in Harrisburg had been. If you could call the dead unhappy.

The case had been complicated only by his forgetfulness. There had been a growth in the patient's throat that had needed to come out. For months Sullivan had campaigned unobtrusively against the man's fear of the knife. He happened to be the banker. When he had given in, everyone in town had known Sullivan was going to operate. The man had bled to death. Sullivan remembered his shattering failure to achieve what a few steps taken in advance would have accomplished, the first step having been to determine whether or not he was hemophilic, a bleeder. But he had slipped right out of his hands, with his wife sobbing and an older surgeon who had been summoned standing by keeping an ethical silence.

But they did not have to tell Sullivan that he had killed

the man, and he had dragged that knowledge into the back-
waters of introspection and lived with it until it dominated
his whole thinking. Until every time he swabbed a throat or
stitched a cut, he thought: *What have I forgotten? Where
have I slipped?* But after a while, when the story had been
around, his problem was solved. There were no more patients. But he had to live and he wanted to lick the thing.
He had come West determined, in a completely new envi-
ronment, to lick it or quit. But he would not be goaded into
a premature attempt by a couple of thoughtless people like
the McFalls.

The patients began to come about seven in the evening.
An old Papago Indian with diseased eyes stumbled in, his
granddaughter leading him. Sullivan did what he could for
the man. Then another and another tapped at the door, a
line formed, and finally anger seized him and he had to re-
strain himself from scattering them with a gunshot. Indian,
Mexican, American, tubercular, epileptic, scabied!

At ten o'clock he turned out the last, extinguished his
lamp, and went to bed. Damn the McFalls!

It started again in the morning. He slipped out the back
door for some breakfast. He ate a plate of salty ham and
eggs, fuming. Four days of it ahead of him before he could
get out of town.

While he was eating, Ed Blocker came into the café. He
spotted him and came across the dirt floor to his table and
sat down, a rumpled, hasty look about him. Sullivan was
wondering what his ailment was when Blocker slipped a
leather-covered notebook before him. "This belong to
you?" It was Sullivan's journal. "Found it by the stage after
you left."

Sullivan thanked him. Blocker remained, ordering a cup

of coffee. A man with the build of a Percheron, he filled his buckskin shirt to tautness and his fingers were large and thick. He had an air of left-handedness. Finally he chuckled.

"You ought to be a stage detective, Doc."

"How's that?"

"I had to read a part of your journal to decide whose it was. Sounds like you've pinned that stage hold-up on poor old Job Martin, the wheat man we passed before the hold-up."

Sullivan smiled. "Just an idea that came to me."

"Well, don't get any of them ideas about me!" Blocker exclaimed. But under his banter was a dark strain of anxiety. "Before we can jail Job for it, we've got to figure out how he could've drove those bulls faster than we traveled in the stage. We passed him three hours before it happened."

It appeared to be a man's natural desire to shield an innocent friend, but Sullivan decided to see how much the joshing Blocker could take. "They could have had horses in the brush."

"A good stage team can always outrun a saddle horse."

"Not in country like that. A horse can take short cuts. They could have ridden over those hills, instead of going around them."

It stopped the stage man. His eyes left Sullivan's. The bare possibility of it seemed to bother him.

At last the doctor chuckled. "I'm not accusing your friend of holding us up. I was curious about his voice and boots being so much like those of the man who led the outlaws, that was all."

Blocker looked relieved. "I just wanted to be sure you didn't go to the marshal with a story like that before you thought it over. . . . See you around, Doc."

All that morning, and into the afternoon, the little side street his room was on was thronged. The satisfaction he should have felt remained at arm's length. He would write a prescription for McFall to fill, and think: *But if this were anything serious*. . . . He would fumble and hesitate until, possibly, it was too late to help. He had lost the ability to make a decision without fumbling.

It was sunset when Tom McFall came in the back way. The bald, florid little druggist was beaming. "Ain't seen such business since the town had the seven-year itch. Katie and me ain't stopped filling prescriptions all day." Sullivan was blue-stoning a cut he had cleaned and did not turn. McFall watched. As the patient left, he spoke gravely. "I guess you meant what you said, didn't you? Well, I reckon that's your business. Tell you what . . . I'll move you over to the hotel tonight and we won't let it out where you are."

"Never mind. As long as I've started, I'll keep on."

After he was in bed, he thought of Ed Blocker again. An odd idea persisted that his anxiety had its roots in guilt. It would have been entirely possible for the alleged wheat merchant and his teamsters to cut ahead, don masks, and stop the stage. The presence of Blocker on the stage when it passed would have told them what they wanted to know— that the strongbox was aboard, the company cash box out of which came a month's salaries and feed bills. Why was Blocker so anxious to protect a friend's good name? Because he himself had given the information that the strongbox would be aboard, in return for a share in the loot? It all made sense, but Sullivan did not see where it was his responsibility to invite his own death by exposing them.

Job Martin arrived in town the following morning with his small train of loaded wagons. Sullivan saw him un-

loading when he went to lunch. He was not surprised when
Martin came to the office later. The wheat man had a deep
brush scratch on his face. He was a tall, slender man with
an indolent grace to his body and a face too proud of itself.
His hair was light brown, going gray, crisp with tight waves.
He wore long sideburns that descended below his ears and
slanted toward his mouth.

"Had a little run-in with a catclaw," he told the doctor
with a crooked grin.

Sullivan sponged the cut with alcohol. It was too clean,
still bearing initial swelling, to be over an hour old. "When
did this happen?" he asked Martin.

"Last night. One of the hazards of the trade." He
donned his hat, and carefully curled the brim, his eyes
probing. "Ed Blocker was telling me something funny. He
says you've got the idea I might have held up that stage.
Me! We liked to died laughing."

"Well, a greenhorn gets odd ideas," Sullivan admitted.
"And, of course, we were all upset."

"I figgered that was it. Just upset. Thought I'd kind of
mention it, though. You know, once a story gets started, it's
hard to stop. I'm not afraid of the law, but I don't want
people pointing at me and sayin' . . . 'There goes that road
agent.' " He laughed heartily, went to the door, and said:
"Well, thanks, Doc. I'll see you around." His steps moved
slowly and without much sureness down the walk.

Through the rest of that day, Sam Sullivan kept open
house to Tucson's infirm. They were beginning to trickle in
from the outlying villages. Once or twice he felt his old confidence, when diagnosis and action came simultaneously,
without the rubbish of self-doubt to wade through. Optimism showed itself, but he ignored it. Sooner or later, there
would come the patient with the internal hemorrhage, the

gangrenous fracture, and the moment he had dreaded would engulf him with its demand for skillful, unhesitating action. Then this fine skin of optimism would split open and the stinking sore beneath would be plain even to a layman.

He put his mind to the problem of Martin and Ed Blocker. He was convinced that the gambit he had started with an entry in his journal had not been played out. Martin had come here with a self-inflicted scratch, and he had gone away still anxious. Somewhere he would be sitting across a table from Ed Blocker. They would be asking over and over the same question: Is he going to talk to anyone before he gets on that stage? What they did about it would depend on the conclusion they reached. At sundown, when the rush of patients had dwindled to an occasional man or woman, he became convinced that there was only one thing they could do—copper their bets.

It was after eight o'clock when he closed, and locked the door. He took pen and ink and inscribed an envelope: **Sheriff, Tucson, T.A.** He set down his suspicions, and sealed the paper in the envelope. As he was about to blow out the lamp before leaving, someone tried the door.

Ed Blocker shouted: "Hey, Doc!"

Sullivan faltered. Somehow the idea of leaving by a back door and scurrying down an alley did not appeal to him. He thrust his Colt under his belt, let his long frock coat cover it, and opened the door. The big section boss stood in the narrow trail of a street. In the moonlight, his flat Stetson hung a long shadow over his blunt features.

"Job for you, Doc. They picked a man up out near Tanque Verde today with a busted wing. Been there a week. The arm's festered so's you can't stay in the same room with him."

104

"Where is he?"

"Over at the depot. Martin's with him now. We've got him ninety percent drunk, so's you can cut if you've got to."

Sullivan hesitated an instant longer. The broken arm, he was convinced, had been achieved by a bullet from his own gun. He had no doubt that Blocker was telling the truth about the man's condition, however, and it was his duty to treat him, even if he sent the sheriff to call on him later. "I'll get my bag," he said.

The stage station was at the corner of Meyer and Alegría Streets. The entrance was on the corner, but Blocker led the way down an alley to a yard in the rear. He crossed this area, and entered a shed beside the stage barn. A dim flame burned in a murky glass chimney. Sullivan's eyes found the sick man under a blanket on a rawhide cot by the far wall.

He was a lean young fellow with long hair and features as white as tallow. A half empty pint of whisky lay in his hand.

Martin, hunched on a box, looked up. "Thanks for coming, Doc. This here's Bill Hamp, one of my 'skinners. He was out hunting and got throwed by his horse."

The stench of decay filled the room. Sullivan looked at the wound, near the right shoulder, and envisioned men who knew nothing of surgery trying to pry a bullet from a man's body, probing deeper and deeper, sowing a harvest of infection. He straightened. "Get some whisky and all the cloths you can find."

The grim overture to horror began, the man Hamp stolidly imbibing frontier anæsthesia. At last he lay in a stupor. Sullivan arranged lamps. He secured his instruments, set out antiseptics, and stood in bitter contemplation of the job ahead.

Suddenly the uprush of terror shook him. He closed his eyes and the muscles of his jaws knotted. The thing leaped up at him, blood grouting from vessels blundering fingers had failed to tie off—the man screaming as the life rushed out of him. Sullivan knew he could not do it. Yet—amazingly—he was doing it. His scalpel was testing the flesh for sensitivity and his voice was saying: "If you'll both catch hold. . . ."

Hamp's screams filled the shed, his blood was everywhere, but the scene did not reach Sullivan. He had slipped back to the days before Harrisburg. His mind and his hands were at work proving themselves. His nerves were bottled up somewhere. Sullivan thought: *That girl!* Locking him up in a disease-rotted village where he was the only physician, the only one who could help them, and, without even knowing what she was doing, making him work it out. Treating a hundred—a hundred?—three hundred patients without loss or blunder, until the old skill and confidence stole back into him, and not even a thing like operating on a man who must certainly die could shake those things from him.

Suddenly he was aware that the man had stopped breathing. He started, bending to inspect the wound. He straightened. "He's gone," he said.

Heavily Blocker murmured: "If he'd had help sooner. . . ."

As the doctor turned to cleanse his instruments, Blocker dropped five gold coins in the stained, ruddy water. Five double eagles. One hundred dollars.

"This is too much," Sullivan said.

Blocker's smile was at once pointed and ingratiating. "Forget it. Forget all about it, Doc. We'll get the undertaker, so's you won't have the bother."

Sullivan dried his hands. "I don't know how it is in Tucson," he said, "but in every other town I know of it's customary for a physician to report any cases of bullet wounds that he handles. I'll have to conform to that rule."

"I wouldn't, Doc," said Job Martin. "I wouldn't bother."

Stiff and silent, Ed Blocker watched him wash his hands, put on his coat, and close his bag. He watched him go to the door, but neither he nor Martin said anything as he went out.

Going back to his room, Sullivan thought: *No one could have saved him.* He examined the thought, surprised. He would have been incapable of it a month ago.

Katie McFall was waiting in his room. She was dressed in a dark gown that pinched in at the waist, plain except for some strategic tucks and a starched white collar and cuffs. She looked fragile and pretty and desirable, but worried.

"Doctor," she said, "I wanted to apologize. I said some things the other day that I've been sorry for ever since. It was none of my business if you didn't want to take patients. And I want to say that. . . ."

Sullivan took her by the shoulders. "Katie, I'm the one to apologize. You were the doctor this time. You didn't know that, did you? But you worked a greater cure on me than I ever worked on a patient."

She appeared puzzled and a bit alarmed.

"Tomorrow I'll tell you all about it," Sullivan said. "I've decided to stay."

"Oh, that's wonderful!"

Sullivan produced the letter he had written. "But right now I want to see that this gets into the sheriff's hands."

Sam Sullivan locked the door after her, and put a chair against it. He could not go over with her for two reasons.

He felt safer within walls, and, if a shot had to be taken at him, he did not want it hitting Katie McFall by accident. He waited what seemed an interminable time in the low, flaring light of the lamp. There were no shades, but the oiled rawhide panes were opaque.

Someone was in the street. After a moment, he went past. Someone else approached, and this man did not pass by, but stopped there in the dark and stood quite still. At the same moment, Sullivan heard footfalls grind cautiously in the rear. He had his Navy Colt in his hand.

One of the rawhide panes bent inward, popped, and exhibited a thin, shining point of steel sliding downward. The pane was ripped thoroughly away and a man shouted: *"¡Vámonos!"* Ed Blocker, one hand holding the stiff rawhide back, stood head and shoulders in the opening.

Sullivan swung the gun to cover him. At the same instant, something struck the rear door shatteringly. It slammed inward, and a man lunged through at a stumbling fall and sprawled on the floor with a shotgun in his hands. Blocker's shot was only an instant away, but the menace of Martin's scatter-gun was more urgent. Sullivan veered the gun barrel, and let the hammer fall. Martin's twelve-gauge filled the whole room with its flash and thunder, extinguishing the lamp and shredding into the cot. But through the ringing in his ears, the doctor heard him groaning.

Ed Blocker's shot laced the darkness redly. The bullet slammed off the adobe wall. Sullivan squeezed the trigger again, but nothing happened. He had forgotten to re-cock. He threw his arm high, brought it down again, the gun cocked this time. He fired once more, and was lowering the gun for a third shot when the sound of the section boss' falling reached him. He stood a long while in the darkness. Then, down the street, he heard them running.

He went out the back door and breathed thirstily of the cool night air. After a while he had the strange thought that he actually owed a debt to the men who had tried to kill him. If they had not dragged him over to operate on a dying man, he might never have put himself to the test. Katie had devised a cure—but they had provided the proof.

A deep vein of satisfaction ran strongly in him. It seemed to color the mean little mud-box village. A man could do more good here than in any pampered city of the East. He could find the kind of wife he needed for the rigors of frontier practice, too. As he went back, Sam Sullivan felt pretty sure he had found the one for him.

Good Loggers Are
Dead Loggers

Harney was relatively sober, yet intoxicated enough to talk with all the eloquence that made him a character in Mountain City. Jim Crockett sat in the print shop with him while Harney tinkered with the Hoe steam press. Crockett was a cattleman and busy with the spring work, but he liked to drop in and listen to Harney's onward and upward talks. Ed Harney was old and bitter enough to be cynical about the mistress who had betrayed him into foolishness and failure, the only mistress he had ever had—the West. He was a drunken old printer and newspaperman who still saw dreams in the coals of an ambition that had brought him from Connecticut to Oregon.

Crockett had started it this morning by mentioning that an Easterner named Mike Latham had tried to buy timber rights on his place last week. "Five thousand a year, Ed," Crockett said. "That beats working for a living."

"If you happen to be short on integrity," Harney remarked.

"Where's integrity come into it?" Jim Crockett demanded.

"Integrity, my boy, is what keeps a man from breeding sons to sell as cattle."

Crockett's grin had a trace of rancor. A blond, brown-skinned young fellow, he had the easy manner of a man with no particular worries. On the ranch he had inherited from his father he had a good living without having to risk his cash in wildcat schemes. He said offhandedly: "I'm too busy to log my own range, Ed. You jobbed me into hiring a gang of tie hacks, but I'm trying to forget that. I still call myself a cattleman."

"Any reason a cattleman can't be smart, as well as smell of cow dung?" Harney demanded. He turned from the hissing, gurgling press. At a type font, his daughter looked around.

"That's telling him, Pop."

Crockett grunted. "What's smart about scattering your fire so you don't know whether you're in cattle or lumbering?"

Harney lurched to the composing bench, his pulpit. He swung the mallet in a crashing blow. "By God, Daniel Boone and Kit Carson would have cut their throats if they knew Westerners would ever come to this!"

Molly Harney's eyes applauded. She was a small and shapely girl of twenty.

"It doesn't worry you," she inquired, "that the only railroad Mountain City is likely to have is owned by a New Yorker? That the stockyards and packing plant are the property of a transplanted Pennsylvanian? Pop shamed you into cutting ties for the railroad trade. It's the nearest thing to integrity I've ever seen you show. It was a start on what this town needs . . . an all-year industry. And yet you can talk about selling your trees . . . the trees that belong to God and not you . . . to Mike Latham!"

Temper began to rise in Jim Crockett. He figured he had done all right without any advice, so far.

"There's nothing wrong with Mike Latham," he growled. "He came over, and we had a couple of drinks and talked business. I practically agreed to do it."

Harney stopped with mallet upraised. He lowered it.

"You . . . you told him . . . ! Molly," he said, "have we still got the sulphur candles we bought that time we had the roaches? We want to fumigate the place after this . . . after Mister Crockett leaves."

Jim stood up. It seemed the Harneys were not such good company this morning. "I've got some things to buy at Ellison's," he said.

The bell over the front door tinkled. Cape Sullivan, who fronted for the Sacramento & Mountain City Railroad and endlessly let the town know he was all for it, pulling shoulder to shoulder with it, although he bought all his supplies in the East, gave them all an arm salute and stepped inside. Two men were with him: Mike Latham, the lumberman, and the woods boss he had brought with him to the ranch the other day, a Basque named Valentine Avala.

Sullivan cupped his ear to the clank and sputter of the printing press. "Sounds prosperous in here!" he exclaimed.

"It always does when the gaskets are shot," Harney said. He had made Sullivan the basis of an editorial one time because of Sullivan's refusal to have company stationery locally printed. His railroad news featured broken schedules and hot boxes.

Sullivan struck his hands together. "Folks, I want you to know a couple of men you'll come to know much better before long. You already know them, Jim. Miss Harney, Ed . . . meet Mike Latham, with Northwestern Lumber. And Mister Avala, his foreman."

"Woods boss," Avala said under his breath.

Harney did not acknowledge the introduction. Latham came forward cordially to shake hands.

Harney looked at his hand, picked up an oilcan, and turned to squirt oil on a bearing. Color surged into Latham's face. Avala swore softly: *"Ivrogne."* But after a

112

moment Latham coughed heavily into his hand, by way of graceful withdrawal. When he confronted the printer again, he betrayed no change.

"Tell you why I came, Mister Harney. We're setting up a field here, you know, and I want the people to be acquainted with my company. I'd like to run a full-page advertisement."

Harney said savagely: "Say it in English! You mean you want to buy me off!" His face was like twisted rawhide. "Get out! Every damned, double-tongued one of you."

Crockett stirred. "Now, look, Ed. . . ."

"Look?" roared the printer. "No, you listen! I came here to help build this country. I saw the foundations laid by honest settlers. Then I saw a pack of Eastern bankers come simpering in. Every resource this country has they took away from us. And now you come into this town I helped settle so's I'd have a place to hide and drink and forget there was such a thing as a broad A. By God, I'll run your ad, and it won't cost you a dime. And you know what it will say? To hell with the Northwestern Lumber Company and its. . . ."

Valentine Avala stepped past Latham and caught the printer by a skinny arm. He would have outweighed him by seventy pounds, although he was four inches shorter. He had his fist pulled back for a blow, but abruptly let Harney free and spat an oath. Harney did a foolish and unexpected thing. He hit the Basque in the face with the oilcan he held. It opened a small cut over the man's eye.

Avala did not exactly hit him. He brought a big, open palm with calluses like half dollars about in a swing. It took Harney on the ear and sent him stumbling into the composing table. He slipped off it, and went down.

Jim Crockett was suddenly between the two of them. He

knew Harney had incited the fight, but it was in him to stand with his own kind. He threw a punch that caught the woods boss on the cheek. Avala bounced off a desk, and came back at the cattleman.

Harney came up from his knees to separate them. "Not in here," he shouted. "You'll break the press!"

Crockett got a look at Ed's face, and he seemed to see a glint of triumph.

Harney said almost whiningly: "Hell of a note to have to let a man do my fighting for me. But that wants rectifyin'. If one thing can still be said of an Oregonian, it's this . . . he'll die before he'll knuckle down to an Easterner! I want Mountain City to see this. It'll be a renewing of our faith in ourselves, a testimonial to the kind of guts that tamed this land. There's a whole street to fight in."

Jim Crockett perceived what had happened. He had been sucked into a fight he didn't want, a fight that would tag him as being the champion of local rights. But Valentine Avala was standing there with his eyes belittling him.

"Tell 'em, then," he said, and shrugged. "I'm going to do some buying at Ellison's. I'll be back in an hour."

Jim was conscious of the coup Harney had achieved. Harney was like a cowbird, attempting to deposit his eggs of ambition in somebody else's nest. Afraid or unable to make the fight himself, he was trying to saddle Crockett with it. A year ago he had persuaded Jim to cut ties for a coast rail-road. It was simple enough, and Jim made money. But it was a side operation, and he wanted to keep it that way. He was a cattleman, start to finish. Molly claimed he was over-cautious. But fortunes grew out of risks, and Jim Crockett was doing all right now.

He was in the dim fragrance of hams and coffee at

Ellison's Mercantile when Peterson, the banker, looked him up.

He said, without too much emphasis: "Hear you're about to expand your lumber business, James. Go to it, boy!"

"I didn't know it, if I am. Ed Harney brought it up, but. . . ."

"Good man, Harney. Wish he drank less. He'd be a local Mark Twain. You take his advice, James. The one thing that will pull this country up is a winter crop. Lumber!"

"You don't seem to get it," Jim began, but the banker was patting his arm and saying: "When the time comes . . . if you're in need of a loan . . . you understand?"

Later, Jim was in the Cascades Bar when Red Rudesill and a dozen ranchers and cowpunchers sought him. Rudesill was a thick-necked, unshaven, towering cattleman.

"So you're going to lick the tar out of that Basco, Avala," Rudesill said.

Jim shrugged. He wished the fight had gone off without Harney's postponing it. It was unpleasant to anticipate a fight after the wine of fury wore off.

"You got to lick him," Rudesill grunted. "He and a gang of his brush rats were in here looking for trouble. He was bragging what he's going to do to you."

"Is that right?"

Crockett absorbed this priming gratefully. He washed it down with two whiskies and topped them with a beer. In a glowering, truculent mood, he heard a man part the half doors and say: "There's a mob of lumber stiffs in front of Harney's you couldn't pound a log wedge through!"

Jim rubbed his hands together. "He's going to cut me into two-foot lengths, is he?"

He walked up the road at the head of a bunch of cowboys that grew as he advanced. A logger sighted them and shouted the word. Out of the mass of woodsmen in their shagged pants and off-breed hats emerged a massive-shouldered figure with dark hair tousled. Valentine Avala stood on the dark earth with his feet widely placed and his fists hanging at his sides.

Avala let Jim come within six feet. Without warning, he ducked his head and rushed him. Jim set himself and swung at his head. He landed a solid blow on the Basque's ear, chopping him to his knees. A roar went up from the cow crowd. Somewhere the voice of Molly Harney reached Jim. It made him feel good, but with the flush of satisfaction still in him he saw Avala lurch up and rush in once more. Jim stabbed and felt the blow slide off a stubbled cheek. Avala's broad, flushed face contorted. He threw a wild blow which, half blocked, still had power to lift Jim off his feet. He stumbled aside over the ruts, the woods boss following with lusty swings. One of them connected with Jim's head, and he went down.

It was the woods crowd that roared now, while the Basque straddled Jim, got a hammerlock and, twisting his neck, began to slug at his face. A shout of disapproval came from Red Rudesill. The punishment shook Jim alive. He began to struggle, but Avala tightened the hold about his neck and smashed a vicious blow into his mouth. The strangling pressure on his neck began to choke him. Suddenly armed with a terror of suffocation, Jim flung up both arms and got a hold about the other's neck. He brought him down and onto his face with a heave, crawled away, and got to his feet before the Basque recovered.

Valentine Avala laughed as he got up. "The little cowboy has enough?" he taunted.

116

Jim walked toward him, feinted, and saw the Basque cover up. Then he slammed one into Avala's belly. Avala gasped and stumbled back, losing color and blowing out a windy curse. He tried to keep Jim away, but Jim sensed that this was as good a moment as he would ever have with this chunky lumberjack who was as tough as a barrel of gristle. But getting next to him was difficult. The man kept moving, pushing him away with both hands, while he fought the sickness of the belly punch. *The hell with ethics!* Jim Crockett thought. Avala had the ethics of a rutting buck. Jim lunged in, linked both hands behind the Basque's head, and pulled his head down. At the same time he brought up his knee. Avala's face and Jim's knee made contact solidly. Avala reeled away.

Suddenly he threw everything into a rush. Jim kept away from him. Avala, bloody and shaken, tried to taunt him into coming within range. Jim dug straight into him with a long overhand punch that terminated in the middle of the woods boss' face. Avala's features loosened. He sank down, but the strong fight instinct in him caused him to roll onto hands and knees and rest there. Jim straddled him and raked a spurred boot back into Avala's thigh. Avala jerked as the tines of Jim's spur cut him. Jim rowelled him like a green broncho. He got off, at last, and stood waiting to see what the woods boss would do. Avala got up somehow, stood there in a sort of slouch for a moment, but all at once caved in.

Jim started to walk away. The road turned on end, and he felt himself reeling. Ed Harney was there to catch one arm, Red Rudesill grabbing the other.

In the *Sentinel* office, Harney sat him in a chair. "We showed 'em, boy! Now you're going to hire a gang of his own loggers and go in there and start cleaning up."

Crockett was too sick to argue it. Molly led him into the parlor of the little log house across the alley from the shop. Here she began washing him up and pulling cuts together with adhesive. He felt better. He had never been so close to her before.

"Like the fight?" he asked her.

"I hated it. But it had to be done, or those loggers would have taken over the whole town. Are you going to follow it up?"

"I don't know."

"I'll bet you could hire some of Latham's own loggers away from him, like Pop says."

Jim said doggedly: "Maybe you two would like to be the lumbermen? I'll lease you the timber rights any time you say."

"I'd look nice in hob-nailed boots, wouldn't I?" she told him. "All I can do is hope to send out some sons to lick this country into shape."

"It's to be all boys, is it?" Jim grinned.

"I thought a couple of each. But what can they do if we sell the things that might have been the basis of their strength?"

Jim got the point. He rose, thinking about it, and for a moment stood curling the brim of his hat. "Well, I'll give it a try."

Molly's face lighted. She reached up to pull his face down to hers and kissed him on the cheek. "Give 'em the devil, Jim."

Jim wandered back down the alley. Even a Harney's kiss had to have a motto tied to it.

Mike Latham was waiting at the livery stable where he had left his horse overnight. He laughed as he looked at Jim. "You and Valentine mixed it proper."

Jim grinned. It was difficult to be stiff with a man of his affability. Latham went into the warm reek of the stable with him and watched him throw the Tipton across his pony. "I had the feeling today that you don't feel as warmly about it as the old man."

"Not quite. But I'm going to have a cut at logging."

Latham's frown lasted only an instant. "Good luck, then. You'll need it. Loggers don't come for what you pay cowpunchers, you know. And the equipment will set you back plenty. I doubt that you'll show a profit for two years."

Jim did not answer.

"However, if you're set on it," Latham said casually, "I think I can make things easier for you. I've bought a ranch over on Blue Creek. I'll start logging it next week. I hate to drag the logs clear around your place to reach the river. I'd like to cut a road through, bring the logs to the river, and snake them out above town, the way you do your ties. I'll pay a hundred a month for an easement."

Jim thought of the country up there around Blue River. Expenses on a log would run to more than the log was worth to get it out, unless it came across his land. "Wouldn't pay for the trees you tore up," he said.

"You'll need the road yourself, Jim. It'd be a favor to you for me to build it. But I can go to one-fifty if you can't see it that way."

"I can't. I'll take three."

Lathan scowled. "If I paid more than two-fifty, they'd fire me. I only work for a living myself, you know."

You smoke good cigars for a working man, Jim thought. "Let's say two-seventy-five and forget about it," he said.

As he turned his pony, Latham said quickly: "I'll have a contract drawn up."

He saw Latham's face as he went out the door. It made

him understand better the way Ed Harney felt.

This was in late April. Jim Crockett was still busy moving cattle from the tired winter range up onto his forest pastures. Licks had to be replenished, calves missed in the weaning roundup branded and vaccinated. He found a logger named Cliff Tuttle willing to work for him as woods boss.

Tuttle was a bandy-legged woodsman of fifty. He had no affection for the log operators, and opened up on Latham one day.

"He's out to get them trees, Jim, one way or another! This is the finest yellow pine stand on the Coast. He ain't building a road, pond, and jammer for what he'll take off Blue Creek. I seen what he did in the redwood country. I hope he don't get away with it here."

The easement checks came in regularly, but, as Jim feared, he found damage to trees and graze. The log road was a path through the woods inclined to vary from twenty feet to a hundred.

Tuttle rode back from town one day. "Better git up there and get a rate from Sullivan. We've got a pond full of logs waiting to be moved."

Jim was nearly broke by this time. He decided to take Peterson up on his offer of a loan. He followed the log road in, through deep stands of pine and fir. At one point a side road had been created. Jim sat a moment in rising fury. There was small doubt where the road led. Angrily he swung toward it. He came out in a saucer-like meadow holding a boxed spring and a dammed earth tank. Bull teams had been watered here, logs had gouged the low wall of the tank until the water broke loose, the grass was rutted by a dozen trails.

It had been one of the spots where Jim liked to pause and think: *This is ranching. This is Oregon.* In a couple of years perhaps he could think those things again. But not until a month's work had been put in on the spring and tank, and not until winter snows and spring thaws had healed the scars. Harney was right. The whole breed was bad. The blood was thin and scrounging. He would tell Latham that.

Just west of town, he passed his pond, a turbid backwater choked with logs. On the bank, between pond and railroad, lurked the greasy carcass of the winch Jim had bought. He rode on to Latham's pond, at the far end of town. A small crew of men was loading logs on a flat car. Latham was not there.

Jim stopped at the bank and got a loan of five thousand dollars, the first loan against the ranch in a generation.

The branch office of the Sacramento & Mountain City Railroad was upstairs in a frame building. Three clerks occupied themselves at bookkeeping, filing, and operating a letter press. Cape Sullivan took Jim into the railed enclosure.

"I've got a pond full of logs now," Jim told him. "I'd like to get them moving. Am I entitled to a rate?"

Sullivan drew a circle on a pad, enclosed it within a square, and dropped the pencil. "The usual discount for cash. But. . . ."

A ripple went down Jim's back.

"I wish you'd talked to me sooner about this. I'm tied up solid with Northwestern."

"What do you mean?"

Sullivan's face pinched. "You can't abuse a narrow-gauge road, or the first thing you know your maintenance exceeds your income. I know exactly how much heavy traffic I can handle. If I were to go beyond that, I'd be having broken rails, blind sags, and all the other what-not of an overworked railroad. Son, I hate to leave you out on a limb, but. . . ."

Jim stood up. "You're a common carrier," he snapped.

Sullivan smiled tolerantly. "It's not so simple as that, my boy. Of course, we can amortize our expenses, borrow from dividends for contingencies. But when you come right down to it. . . ."

Jim leaned over the desk to take hold of Sullivan's stock. He hauled him out of the chair. "When you come right down to it, you and Latham decided this was as good a way as any to bring me to heel!"

He shoved him away. Aware of the glances of his employees, Sullivan said: "You can't lick us the way you did Valentine Avala. You're going up against the law when you come in here threatening bodily injury."

"Did I threaten you?" Crockett snarled. "Well, I can't back down on a thing like that." Jim reached across to pluck Sullivan's glasses from his nose, throw them on the floor, and slap the railroad man with the back of his fist. Sullivan reeled back and stumbled over his chair. He went down, and lay there on his back.

"You're makin' a regular alley fighter out of me," Jim complained.

Still in this mood, he stopped at Harney's. The printer was putting new gaskets in the steam press. Molly was in back, locking up a page of type. Harney's cynical old hawk's face broke into pleasant lines.

"You boycotting us, Jim?"

"Sullivan just refused to handle my freight!" Jim blurted.

Harney was a contradictory one. Jim had expected rage,

but the printer merely grunted. "You didn't expect to make a fortune without working for it, did you?"

"After all," Molly told him, "a fight is a fight."

"Then I wish it was your fight. Latham's torn up half my range with his ox teams, Sullivan won't let me ship my logs, and Peterson squeezes nine percent interest out of me."

Harney shrugged. "It ain't our fault if you gave Mike Latham an easement. That was the stupidest thing you've done yet."

"The stupidest thing I ever did was to let you talk me into trying to be a logger." He started out.

"What are you going to do?" Molly demanded.

"Whatever looks easiest. Maybe I'll sell out to Latham."

On the way back, he swung past the meadow and found six bull teams being watered by a dozen muleskinners. Jim pulled the carbine from the saddle boot, and fired a shot that startled the muleskinners.

"Get those brutes out of here!" he shouted. "Leave the logs. Find another way back to camp. The next bull team I catch on my land will be a dead bull team."

He fired a second shot into the ground near them. The bullwhackers began to chouse the yoked animals back up the trail to the main road. Jim wheeled his horse, and rode toward Mike Latham's logging camp.

Where Latham's crews had cut across the old Chandler Ranch in Blue Creek, the camp was in a vast field of stumps and torn earth. Bull teams were penned in pole corrals. Tarpaper shacks housed workers and equipment. Latham came from a door to wave at him. Jim went into the shack with him.

Valentine Avala was laboring over a report of some kind, his thick fingers clumsily wielding a stub pencil. He sat hunched over his slab desk, staring unsmilingly at Jim. The memory of a day in Mountain City was in his eyes.

"What are you doing out there?" Jim asked him. "Getting ready to put in a crop?"

Latham chuckled. "Valentine's pretty thorough, at that."

The Basque swirled whisky in a cup. "No sense in wasting good timber."

"I thought there were laws about how much timber you could cut in one area."

"It evens out. I leave more, where there's more new growth."

"Is this the way you'd have logged my place?"

Latham shrugged. "Your cattle don't eat trees, do they? Besides, those things can be taken care of in a contract."

"The way you took care of my graze and springs?"

"Some of the 'whackers have been a little careless. But I figured that for two-seventy-five a month. . . ."

Suddenly Jim struck out at the cup on the desk, shattering it against the stove. Avala's hands dropped to his lap. "I don't give a damn how you figure! You can figure you're licked here, if you've got to cross my land to operate. I just ran off six of your bull teams from the spring in Stone Meadow. You've ruined the spring and most of the grass. Harney was right . . . you can't deal with an Easterner without getting his smell on you."

Latham had that look on his face again. Underlying it was a turgid malevolence. "A contract is a contract," he declared.

"And a Thirty-Thirty is a Thirty-Thirty. I'll bet I can throw a slug farther with a carbine than you can with a contract."

He turned to the door, but halted with his hand on the

knob to say to Avala, who had moved sidewise on the chair: "Watch it, Basco. I've got a lot of nice skins on the floor of my cabin. You'd fit in so well they'd think I shot you out of a tree."

Avala brought his hands into sight again.

Red Rudesill was at the cabin when Crockett reached home. Rudesill seldom made a trip to or from town without spending a night with Jim. The six foot four cattleman had carved steaks from a loin he had found hanging in the cooler. He had made coffee, piled thick slices of bread on the table, and set fried potatoes and onions to filling the cabin with their fragrance. Cliff Tuttle came in from the logging camp just before they sat down.

"Sullivan fired his cannon today," Jim snapped. "He won't carry my lumber."

Tuttle rubbed his jaw with a stubby, tattooed hand. "The dirty cinder-lovin' son-of-a-bitch! It's ag'in' the law, Jim."

"But by the time I prove it, I'll be cleaned out. I had to borrow five thousand to keep going. How long will that last, with nothing coming in?"

Strong emotion, in himself or others, embarrassed Red Rudesill. He stirred four spoons of sugar slowly into his coffee. "I've got a couple thousand put by, Jim. It's yours when you need it."

"That's how Latham would want it," Jim said. "The more of you I can drag down with me, the more timber rights he's going to pick up on sacrifice sales."

They were silent for a while. "The river's the best thing you've got," Tuttle declared. "We can float the logs down to the valley. Then it would only mean snaking them about ten miles over to the trunk." He squinted at the smoky ceiling. "A dozen boys to walk the river and keep 'em moving. Another crew of bullwhackers. Going to come high, Jim, but what else can you do?"

Jim said: "Nothing. But it will be nice to know that Latham's having to detour, too. As long as they're still making shells, he's going to do it."

In four weeks he had gone through three thousand dollars of the bank loan. Tuttle had a sluggish serpent of logs creeping down the river. Loggers walked the banks, keeping the timber moving. Bullwhackers snaked them from the new pond across the low foothills to the trunk line. But it was primitive work. The mill checks that reached Jim were small. The brag he had made in haste he was repenting at leisure.

Tuttle claimed Latham was having his worries, too. Mountains of logs piled up in the forest, but the pond at Mountain City was empty.

"He's a top nut in the company," Tuttle declared, "but he's got to produce to hold his job. If we can hang on till winter. . . ."

One day the news came up that the logs had jammed below town. Tuttle took it somberly. He put dynamite in his saddlebags before they rode out.

They made Mountain City by dark. It had been Jim's custom to sleep in the print shop when he was in town, but this time he bunked at the hotel. In the morning they rode on and found the jam at a sharp kink in the stream. The logs had jammed in a dirty brown mass. Packed with branches and rocks, they formed a dam that raised the level of the stream behind it and created a pressure to clamp every log tightly. Tuttle wagged his head. He dismounted, threw the saddlebags of dynamite over his shoulder, and started down near the bosque.

Five men were working at the jam. Bull teams stood under yoke nearby. One of the loggers came teetering across the logs to shore. "Locked tighter'n a safe," he said.

Tuttle's temper was close to the surface. "What do you monkeys do when I'm not around, pick the seam squirrels off each other?"

"This is a tough bend to break."

"The trick," Tuttle snapped, "is not to let a jam start. I don't give us a chance in ten." He placed his charge, strung fuse, and directed them out of range.

The logs blew high, twisting slowly in a fountain of dirty water. The jolt was hardly felt in the ground. They heard, rather than saw, the slow stirring of the logs, the deep bass note of grinding timbers. Then a stick moved slowly in a short arc. A jet of water burst from the head of the jam. The whole front crumbled. Logs began to leap forward in the rush of escaping water. Tuttle relaxed. "She goes!"

But after the level of the river sank to normal, three half-submerged logs remained. "Now, why are *them* sticks hanging back thataway?" Tuttle demanded.

The logs rode the currents, twisting slowly. "Get a chain on that closest one," he ordered.

They got a bight around the log. The oxen were barely able to bring the log out of the stream. As it slid across the sand, Jim saw that a cable was cinched tightly about the middle of the log. At the end of it, about twenty feet from the log, dragged a barrel of cement. Two short lengths of rail pierced the barrel, making a rude anchor.

Tuttle said softly: "There's our log jam. Logging ain't tough enough . . . Latham has to make our jams for us."

It was about noon. As they climbed the bank again, they heard a distant hoot of a locomotive. One of Latham's infrequent loads of logs would be along soon. The idea was spontaneous. Jim looked at Cliff Tuttle.

"Yeah, I've got a couple of sticks left." Tuttle grinned.

They reached the railroad tracks a few hundred yards east, left their horses in the jack pines, and jammed the dynamite under a rail. Tuttle struck a match, and came running back to where Jim waited. The explosion was a flat stroke on the warm air. A column of dust ascended. They saw the shallow hole in the grade. Ties were displaced and a rail was bent upward.

The pound and chuff of the locomotive came closer. Sullivan's little 460 was making good time. They saw the smoke rising in impatient plumes above the trees. The sweating engine came in sight. Almost immediately a jet of steam erupted from the whistle. The brake shoes clamped.

But there were flats loaded with sodden logs behind the locomotive, logs with the inertia to bear forward despite the resistance of skidding iron. The fireman leaped through the door. They glimpsed the engineer departing by the opposite one. Drivers locked, the engine slid along the rails, struck the disrupted section hard, and lurched from the iron. There was a sound of boiling water bursting from a broken pipe, an angry rush of live steam. Logs shook on the flats. The rusted vent atop the caboose broke loose. The work engine jolted along the earth, firebox spilling hot cinders, cord wood leaping from the agitated tender. It continued on its way until it reached a cairn of boulders at a bend. Here it piled headlong into the rocks with a clang of metal.

There was an instant of comparative silence. From the caboose jumped a scared man with a vest over his pleated shirt, his spectacles hanging from one ear. Cape Sullivan ran a little way from the crummy and stood waiting for the second man who jumped from the rear platform. Mike Latham was shaken but unfrightened, a large, capable-looking man in breeches and a plaid shirt. He stood watching the crewmen come back to examine the wreckage.

Jim had a lift of exultation. He could not have planned it better.

He heard Latham roaring. "What did you think you were running?"

He and Sullivan walked down the grade. As Jim rode from the trees, he heard the engineer say curtly: "One of the rails was broken. This wasn't no accident, Mister Latham."

Then they saw the pair riding at an easy trot from the jack pines. All of them stood staring as Jim and Tuttle reined in.

"Say, this is bad luck, ain't it?" Jim declared.

Latham had his broad face under control. "It looks that way now. I don't know who will lose most by it in the end, though." His deep-socketed eyes regarded Jim steadily. They had changed in the last few weeks, acquiring smudges beneath them, sobering and hardening. "I'm not a patient man, Jim," he said. "I've been patient with you longer than with most men. This may be the last time you and I ever talk together. I'd like it to be a frank talk." He nodded at the caboose. "Will you talk to me for five minutes?"

The caboose was littered with broken crockery, ashes from the upset stove, and articles hurled from a cupboard. A suitcase lay near a bunk.

"Going on a little trip?" Jim asked.

"Salem. On business."

"Sure it wasn't Sacramento . . . to see if you still have a job?"

"I said I wanted to be frank. I'll start out by admitting that you haven't done my stock with the company any good. Northwestern is accustomed to sending me out on a job and getting it done. It's cost me thirty-five thousand dollars a month to fight you."

"You ought to be about ready to quit."

"I'm just ready to start. I've finally learned something. You and I can't work as rivals. Only one of us is going to log this country."

"Seems like we reach conclusions about the same time," Jim said. "I figure I'm going to be the one, because you're not going to be able to get your logs out after today. I'm going to fill the upper river so full of snags you'll have to send a canoe with every log to get it through."

"We can sit here throwing boasts at each other all day," Latham snapped. "But I'm going to make it simple. I want to buy you out. I'll get you fifteen thousand."

"Can't hear you," Jim said.

Once more Latham had that aristocratic lift to the corner of his mouth. In a temper-shot voice, he said: "Twenty, then! That's the best offer you'll ever get, and it's the last offer you'll get from me."

Jim walked to the platform. "Northwestern hasn't enough money to buy me out. As far as Sullivan goes, I'll build my own spur. Sure, that takes money. But Mountain City's about to grow out of its short pants. I'm going to incorporate. You never thought of that, did you? Why should I keep a good thing all to myself? I'll sell stock, get myself elected president. Why . . . why, by God . . . !" Imagination was getting out of hand. It was striking roots of fire into his brain. He stood there, running his fingers through his hair. "Hell, there's no reason I can't log other men's land when I get through with my own, is there?"

He went down two steps. Latham was behind him on the platform, his mouth an inverted crescent cut like a scar into his face. "Did you think you were fighting only me?" he said. "You're fighting a company that could buy out the state of Oregon. We're going to break you."

"Come around to Harney's print shop tomorrow. We'll have some stock ready to sell by then."

Ed Harney was drunker than Jim Crockett had seen him in some time. Molly was operating the Hoe press, the gasket spitting angrily. Harney sat on a box with an oilcan in his hand, staring at the floor as Jim came in.

He got up, and somberly gripped Jim's hand. "Sorry, Jim," he choked. "I . . . I heard about it."

"Heard about what?"

"The log jam. And about you bein' broke, washed up. Jim, it's your fault, mine and Molly's, and I'm going to sell this shack and broken-down junk shop for what I can get and turn it over to you. Then you can go back to your own trade."

Jim squinted at him. "Any time you start preachin' backward and downward, you're worse'n drunk. You're the only man this town's ever had. Quit? I aim to be the biggest lumber and cattleman Oregon ever saw before I'm through! Listen to me. I've got a mountain of logs up there above town and no way in hell to move them fast enough to feed myself. But I feel like the man who discovered Oregon must have felt. I've been blowing up trains, Ed. Greatest thrill in the world."

Harney came up off the box. "They'll hang you!"

"Nobody hurt. And I just had a talk with Latham. He wants to give me twenty thousand for the place."

"Take it!" Harney screeched. "Don't you know by now you can't lick him? A good big man can always lick a good little man. We're little. The whole damn' Pacific Coast is little. You and me and Molly, even Pete Peterson. But the important thing is to see this country opened up. I just realized that. It don't matter what happens to us. We'll be the butlers and carriage boys and privy diggers . . . but, by George, we'll be part of it."

Jim shook his head. "You've got to get him off that stuff," he told Molly. He began grabbing in the shelves that housed Harney's paper supply. "Got any banknote stock?"

Harney closed one eye. "What do you want with stock certificates?"

"I'm going to incorporate. Ten dollars a share. The Crockett, Harney, Rudesill, and Mountain City Lumber Company."

Harney tromped back to the shelves and grubbed until he found some imitation parchment. "This'll git it! And I've got some gold ink and ornaments to dress 'em up with. Molly, run off a notice . . . seventy-two point Gothic, red ink, use the coated stock. We'll sell the damn' things as fast as they come off the press."

This was near sundown. A half hour after Jim posted the notice, a file of men began to form in front of the *Sentinel* office. It grew until Jim counted thirty-five cattlemen, cowpunchers, loggers, and townsmen. Peterson, the bearded patriarch of the town, crowded into line to demand two thousand dollars' worth of stock.

About eight o'clock Mike Latham appeared briefly with Cape Sullivan and Valentine Avala. They stared at the phenomenon for a short interval, turned, and disappeared into the office of the Sacramento & Mountain City. Jim saw this. He went out back to where his horse was picketed, and brought his carbine inside. He got Cliff Tuttle to sit on the porch of the Harney house and keep the alley clear. Then he returned to the front of the print shop. They had seventy-two hundred dollars in a tin cash box by now.

It was close to nine when Avala returned. He came along the walk with a gang of lumberjacks from the saloons, treading the boardwalk so quietly that Jim did not perceive them until they were within fifty feet. He stepped from the door, and stood in the middle of the walk.

Avala stopped, spreading his arms to halt the others. His face was a shadow under the brim of his hat. Jim said: "How many of you want to buy stock? Let's get going on this."

Avala, a man to take orders rather than to think for himself, cleared his throat. "We were . . . coming for a look," he said.

"Had one?"

Avala turned his head. "Better break it up, boys. Some of these dodos might think we was looking for trouble."

"Sure might," Jim said. "Especially if you don't drop these scantlings."

The Basque tossed his billiard cue away, turned, and left the street. When the loggers had left, Jim Crockett went inside. He told the sweating, shirtless specter at the press: "They're licked. I called Avala's bluff. By tomorrow morning this money will be buried in Peterson's safe and Latham's bluff will be buried with it."

It was the first time he had under-figured Mike Latham since the whole thing started. Near midnight, when the rush was over and they were tying the cash in bundles, someone shouted: *"Fire!"*

They ran out. The flames were consuming a bunk of logs stacked along the river above town. Jim stood with some others who had appeared half-clad to stare down an alley that debouched into the vacant lots mounting the slope to the railroad. Jim did not worry about the logs, but the stakes that held them. They were four-by-fours just high enough to hold the bottom log of each bunk.

Someone was hanging on the rope in the volunteer firehouse. Men began to shove their shirt tails in trousers and start off.

He ran to the print shop and found a crowbar. As he sprinted out the back door, he saw the fire soar forty feet above the bunk in a sudden surge. Then he saw something else. A figure near the logs who came into view briefly to swing an axe at one of the restraining stakes. His shoulders pivoted three times. There was a shifting in the log pile. The bottom log shot forward, angularly. Then the other side of it broke loose, and it leaped down the slope at an angle that would take it toward the east end of town.

Jim stood there, paralyzed. He watched to see the log extinguish itself by the action of rolling, but little pockets of fire continued to appear. Then he was aware of the rest of the pile coming in a swerving, leaping horde. Like hell on wheels.

The fire company was racing around the corner of Ellison's Mercantile. When the men saw the logs thundering toward them, they tried to veer the hand engine back toward the street. It fell onto its side. They dragged it away, and then deserted to run for safety. A fifteen-hundred-footer crashed into the frail pump cart, and rumbled on. It plunged into the back of the Mercantile and went halfway through the wall. The flames it had nearly shaken loose in its flight surged up again.

When Avala saw him, his hand went down to the holster at his side. Jim's arm drew back, and he hurled the crowbar like a lance. The Basque tried to duck it, but fell. Twisting, the bar struck him flat across the side. He shouted his pain, and staggered up with the Colt in his hand. Jim sprawled.

The double stroke of the gun jolted against his eardrums. He had the good sense to lie there. After an instant, the woods boss ran on, his left hand clamped to his ribs.

The first building to go down was Ellison's. After that, there was no keeping track of the casualties. Harney's home was ablaze, but Jim found Molly and Ed in the shop, gathering the things most important to them, the cash box, some papers, a font of type. He helped them carry these things into the street, and went back to see whether the hand press could be moved. With the help of some others, they got it into the street.

With only Riordan's Saloon and the bank still secure, Jim Crockett, Ed Harney, and Tuttle slipped away to bury the corporation money. Harney shoved the last of the earth into the hole they dug, as though he were burying an old friend.

"I didn't know it was in the Lord to be so mortal mean," he said tragically.

"I'm not sure He was," Jim told him. "I caught Avala cutting the logs loose. Ed, if we ever want a comeback on this, we've got to find him. . . ."

Tuttle grunted. "Not going to be easy."

Harney's eyes glittered in the last light of the fire. Despoiling hands had been laid on the thing he loved, this mountain town the map makers had hardly heard of. More than an editorial would be required to avenge a fire-gutted town. "Latham's office," he said. "He'd be with the critter that sent him out to do it."

"Not if Latham could help it. Avala's marked. But we can look."

Latham's town headquarters was a small log shack near his pond. It was dark, beyond the light of the flames, untouched and empty. One possibility was eliminated. "What about Sullivan's?" Tuttle suggested.

"It's gone. Nothing left but the bank and saloon now," Harney grunted.

Jim touched his arm. "Isn't that Latham's caboose on the siding?"

Harney's plates rattled. "By God! And a light!"

They could hear talk as they closed in on the battered red caboose. Jim hated to hear what was being said. Latham's voice was barely audible.

". . . No damned excuse for coming back here! Even if you'd had your arm shot off. I told you! The hand car's waiting. Take it and get the hell out!"

Avala sounded dead beat. "I can't operate no hand car, boss! My ribs . . . there ain't a sound one on my right side."

Jim had given Ed the carbine he had carried from the print shop before it fell. He had his Frontier model Colt. He put his weight carefully on the step, but the car tipped slightly, and the conversation ended abruptly. There was no use trying to be cagey. He lunged against the door and sent it crashing back.

Before him was a cramped view of the bunk-lined interior he had visited before. Near the door stood Avala, his shirt soaked with blood, his hair rumpled. There was a gun under his belt, and his hand was already on it as Jim caught at a bunk. Latham was standing at a table covered with papers—stark, bearded, intent. Latham grabbed a revolver from the table, and ducked beneath it. Cape Sullivan, the greedy, the pliable, stood against the far door as if nailed there. His voice was like a woman's scream.

"*No, Jim!* Just Latham! I begged him not to!"

Avala stood not eight feet from Jim. He went on tugging the gun from his belt, a single-minded man who did not know where heroism ended.

Avala, bloody and sweating, the whites of his eyes glassy, pulled back the hammer. Jim let his fall. His arm was kicked high by the recoil. He cocked again as he brought the gun down. Avala had dropped his Colt. He was out of it. Latham, beneath the table, suddenly hurled it at Jim and, crouching there, fired upward. The shot struck a leg of the table and cast splinters into Jim's face.

Harney was yelling: "My buck!" He lunged past Jim, firing the carbine as he went. Levering another shell into the chamber and firing once more, Latham dropped his gun and came to his knees. His face was twisted darkly. He extended his hand toward the printer in a blind gesture, but let it fall after a moment, and sagged forward.

Sullivan still stood against the door. He was white as cloth. He looked as though he might faint, but he was still able to talk. "His idea, Jim. Whole thing. I'll carry your freight, always did want to."

"We may throw a little business your way," Ed Harney said. "Chances are we'll build our own road through. . . . Let's get out where the air's fresh," he said suddenly.

They walked slowly back toward town, toward the job they would be months finishing. But the realization was coming to Jim that Latham had done the one thing that would unite the town so solidly an outsider couldn't drive a wedge into its economy.

"We've got a bank, a printing press, and a saloon," Ed Harney exulted. "What more does a town need?"

Jim's thinking had gone far ahead. He saw Molly, waiting for them at the dark hulk of the printing press, and said: "A preacher." He hurried ahead. A man couldn't wait all night for something like this. . . .

Burn Him Out!

Will Starrett squatted before the campfire in the creek bottom, drinking his coffee and watching the other men over the rim of his tin cup. In the strong light from the fire, the sweat and the dirt and the weariness made harsh masks of their faces. They were tired men. But pushing up through their fatigue was a growing restlessness. Now and then a man's face was lost in heavy shadow as he t   away to talk with a neighbor. A head nodded vigorously, and the buzz of talk grew louder. To Starrett, listening, it was like the hum a tin of water makes as it comes to a boil. The men were growing impatient now and drawing confidence from each other. Snatches of talk rose clearly. Without the courtesy of direct address, they were telling Tim Urban what to do.

Starrett swirled his cup to raise the sugar from the bottom and studied Urban coldly. The man leaned against the wheel of a wagon, looking cornered. He held a cup of coffee in his hand and his puffy face was mottled with sweat and dirt. On his hands and forearms was the walnut stain of grasshopper excrement. He was a man for whom Starrett felt only mild contempt. Urban was afraid to make his own decisions and yet unable to accept outside advice. The land on which he stood, and on which they had worked all day, was Urban's. The decision about the land was his, too. But because he hesitated, so obviously, other voices were growing strong with eagerness to make up his mind for him. Tom Cowper was the most full-throated of the twenty-five

138

who had fought the grasshoppers since dawn.

"If the damned poison had only come!" he said. "We could have been spreading it tonight and maybe had them stopped by noon. Since it ain't come, Tim. . . ." He scowled and shook his head. "We're going to have to concoct some other poison just as strong."

"What would that be?" Starrett struck a match, and shaped the orange light with his hands.

Cowper, a huge man with a purplish complexion, badger-gray hair, and tufted sideburns, pondered without meeting Starrett's eyes and answered without opening his mind. "Well, we've got no time to think of something, or they'll eat this country right down to bedrock. We're only three miles from your own land right now. The 'hoppers didn't pasture on Urban's grass because they liked the taste of it. They just happened to land here. Once they get a start, or a wind comes up, they'll sweep right down the valley. We've got to stop them here."

Will Starrett looked at him and saw a big, angry-eyed man worrying about his land as he might have worried about any investment. To him, land was a thing to be handled like a share of railroad stock. You bought it when prices were low; you sold it when prices were high. Beyond this, there was nothing to say about it.

When Starrett did not answer him, Cowper asked: "What is there to do that we haven't already done? If we can't handle them here on Tim's place, how can we handle them on our own?"

They all knew the answer to that, Starrett thought. Yet they waited for someone else to say it. It was Tim Urban's place to speak, but he lacked the guts to do it. Starrett dropped the match and tilted his chin as he drew on the cigarette. The fire's crackling covered the far-off, infinite rattling of the grasshoppers; the night covered the sight of them. But they were still there in every man's mind, a hated, crawling plague sifting the earth like gold-seekers. They were there with their retching green smell and their racket, as of a herd of cattle in a dry cornfield. Across two miles of good bunch grass land they had squirmed, eating all but a few weeds, stripping leaves and bark from the trees. They had dropped from the sky upon Urban's home place the night before, at the end of a hot July day. They had eaten every scrap of harness in the yard, gnawed fork handles and corral bars, chewed the paint off his house, and left holes where onions and turnips had been in his garden. By night, four square miles of his land had been destroyed, his only stream was coffee-colored with hopper excrement, and the glistening brown insects called Mormon crickets were moving on toward the valley's heart as voraciously as though wagonloads of them had not been hauled to a coulée all day and cremated in brush fires. No man knew when a new hatch of them might come across the hills.

Starrett frowned. He was a dark-faced cattleman with a look of seasoned toughness, a lean and sober man, who in his way was himself a creature of the land. "Well, there's one thing," he said.

"What's that?" Cowper asked.

"We could pray."

Cowper's features angered, but it was his foreman, Bill Hamp, who gave the retort. "Pray for seagulls, like the Mormons?"

"The Mormons claim they had pretty good luck."

With an angry flourish, Hamp flung the dregs of his coffee on the ground. He was a drawling, self-confident Missourian with truculent pale eyes and a brown mustache. The story was that he had marshaled some cow town a few years ago, or had been a gunman in one of them. He had been Cowper's ramrod on his other ranches in New Mexico and Colorado, an itinerant foreman who suited Cowper. He did all Cowper asked of him—kept the cows alive until the ranch could be resold at a profit. To Hamp, a ranch was something you worked on, from month to month, for wages. Land, for him, had neither beauty nor dimension. But he could find appreciation for something tangibly beautiful like Tom Cowper's daughter, Lynn. Because Starrett himself had shown interest in Lynn, Bill Hamp hated him— hated him because Starrett was in a position to meet her on her own level.

Hamp kept his eyes on Starrett. "If Urban ain't got the guts to say it," he declared, "I have. Set fires! Burn the 'hoppers out!" He made a sweeping gesture with his arm.

Around the fire, men began to nod. Urban's rabbity features quivered. "Bill, with the grass dry as it is, I'd be burned out!"

Hamp shrugged. "If the fire don't get it, the 'hoppers will," he said.

Cowper sat there, slowly nodding his head. "Tim, I don't see any other way. We'll backfire and keep it from getting out of hand."

"I wouldn't count on that," Starrett said.

"It's take the risk or accept catastrophe," Cowper declared. "As far as its getting out of hand goes, there's the county road where we could stop it in a pinch."

"Best to run off a strip with gang plows as soon as we set the fires," Hamp said. He looked at Starrett with a hint of humor. Downwind from Tim Urban's place at the head of the valley was Starrett's. Beyond that the other ranches sprawled over the prairie. Hamp was saying that there was no reason for anyone to buck this, because only Urban

141

could lose by the fire.

Starrett said nothing, and the opinions began to come.

Finally Cowper said: "I think we ought to take a vote. How many of you are in favor of setting fires? Let's see hands on it."

There were twenty men in the creek bottom. Cowper counted fourteen in favor. "The rest of you against?"

All but Starrett raised their hands. Hamp regarded him. "Not voting?"

"No. Maybe you'd like to vote on a proposition of mine."

"What's that?"

"That we set fire to Cowper's ranch house first."

Cowper's face contorted. "Starrett, we've got grief enough without listening to poor jokes!"

"Burning other men's grass is no joke. This is Urban's place, not yours or mine. I'm damned if any man would burn me out by taking a vote."

Bill Hamp sauntered to the wagon, and placed his foot against a wheel hub. "Set by and let ourselves be eaten out . . . is that your idea?"

"Ourselves?" Starrett smiled.

Hamp flushed. "I may not own land, but I make my living from it."

"There's a difference, Hamp. You need to sweat ten years for a down payment before you know what owning an outfit really means. Then you'd know that, if a man would rather be eaten out than burned out, it's his own business."

Hamp regarded him stonily and said: "Are you going to stand there and say we can't fire the place to save the rest?"

Starrett saw the men's eyes in the firelight, some apprehensive, some eager, remembering the stories about Bill

Hamp and his cedar-handled .45. "No," he said. "I didn't say that."

Hamp, after a moment, let a smile loosen his mouth.

But Starrett was saying: "I've got nothing against firing, but everything against deciding it for somebody else. Nobody is going to make up Urban's mind for him, unless he agrees to it."

Urban asked quickly: "What would you do, Will?"

It was not the answer Starrett wanted. "I don't know," he said. "What are you going to do?"

Urban knew an ally when he saw one. He straightened, spat in the fire, and with his thumbs hooked in the riveted corners of his jeans pockets stared at Cowper. "I'm going to wait until morning," he said. "If the poison don't come . . . and if it don't rain or the wind change . . . I may decide to fire. Or I may not."

Information passed from Cowper to Bill Hamp, traveling on a tilted eyebrow. Hamp straightened like a man stretching slowly and luxuriously. In doing this, his coat was pulled back and the firelight glinted on his cartridge belt. "Shall we take that vote again, now that Mister Starrett's finished stumping?" he asked.

Starrett smiled. "Come right down to it, I'm even principled against such a vote."

Hamp's dark face was stiff. The ill-tempered eyes held the red catch lights of the fire, but he could not phrase his anger for a moment.

Starrett laughed. "Go ahead," he said. "I've always wondered how much of that talk was wind."

Cowper came in hastily. "All right, Bill! We've done all we can. It's Urban's land. As far as I'm concerned, he can fight the crickets himself." He looked at Starrett. "We'll know where to lay the blame if things go wrong."

He had brought seven men with him. They got up, weary, unshaven cowpunchers wearing jeans tied at the bottoms to keep the grasshoppers from crawling up their legs. Cowper found his horse and came back, mounted.

"You'll be too busy to come visit us for a while." His meaning was clear—he was speaking of his daughter. "As for the rest of it . . . I consider that a very dangerous principle you've laid down. I hope it never comes to a test when the 'hoppers have the land next to *mine*."

They slept a few hours. During the night a light rain fell briefly. Starrett lay with his head on his saddle, thinking of the men he had so nearly fought with. Cowper would sacrifice other men's holdings to protect his own. That was his way. Urban would protest feebly over being ruined with such haste, but he would probably never fight. Hamp was more flexible. His actions were governed for the time by Cowper's. But if it came to a showdown, if the grasshoppers finished Urban and moved a few miles east onto Starrett's land, this dislike that had grown into a hate might have its airing.

Starrett wished Cowper had been here longer. Then the man might have understood what he was trying to say. That land was not shares of stock, not just dirt with grass growing on it. It was a bank, a feed lot, a reservoir. The money, the feed, the water were there as long as you used them wisely. But spend them prodigally, and they vanished. Your cattle gaunted down, your graze died. You were broke. But after you went back to punching cows or breaking horses, the grass came back, fine as ever, for a wiser cowman to manage.

It was a sort of religion, this faith in the land. How could you explain it to a man who Gypsied around taking up the slack in failing ranches by eliminating extra hands, dispensing with a useless horse herd, and finally selling the thing at a profit? Ranching was a business with Cowper and Hamp, not a way of life.

Just at dawn the wind died. The day cleared. An hour later, as they were riding, armed with shovels into the blanket of squirming 'hoppers to shovel tons of them into the wagons and dozers, a strong wind rose. It was coming from the north, a warm, vigorous breeze that seemed to animate the grasshoppers. Little clouds of them rose and flew a few hundred yards and fell again. Slowly the earth began to shed them, the sky absorbed their rattling weight, and they moved in a low cloud toward the hills. Soon the land was almost clean. Where they had passed in their crawling advance, the earth was naked with only a few clumps of brush and skeletal trees left.

Urban leaned on the swell of his saddle with both elbows. He swallowed a few times. Then he said softly, like a man confessing a sin: "I prayed last night, Will. I prayed all night."

"Then figure this as the first installment on an answer. But this is grasshopper weather. They're coming out of the earth by the million. Men are going to be ruined if they come back out of the brush, and, if the wind changes, they will. Don't turn down that poison if it comes."

That day Starrett rode into Antelope. From the stationmaster he learned that Tim Urban's poison had not come. A wire had come instead, saying that the poison had proved too dangerous to handle and suggesting that Urban try Epsom salts. Starrett bought all the Epsom salts he could find—a hundred pounds. Then he bought a ton of rock salt and ordered it dumped along the county road at the southwest border of his land.

He had just ridden out of the hot, shallow cañon of the

town and turned down toward the river when he saw a flash of color on the bridge, among the elms. He came down the dusty slope to see a girl in green standing at the end. She stood turning her parasol as she watched him drop the bridle reins and come toward her.

"Imagine!" Lynn smiled. "Two grown men fighting over grasshoppers!"

Will held her hand, warm and small in the fragile net of her glove. "Well, not exactly. We were really fighting over foremen. Hamp puts some of the dangedest ideas in Tom's head."

"The way I heard it some ideas were needed last night."

"Not that kind. Hamp was going to ram ruination down Urban's throat."

"You have more tact than I thought," she told him. "It's nice of you to keep saying Hamp. But isn't that the same as saying Tom Cowper?"

He watched the creek dimple in the rain of sunlight through the leaves. "I've been hoping it wouldn't be much longer. I could name a dozen men who'd make less fuss and get more done than Hamp. If Urban had made the same suggestion to your father, Hamp would have whipped him."

She frowned. "But if Urban had had the courage, he'd have suggested firing himself, wouldn't he? Was there any other way to protect the rest of us?"

"I don't think he was as much concerned about the rest of us as about himself. You've never seen wildfire, have you? I've watched it travel forty miles an hour. July grass is pure tinder. If we'd set fires last night, Tim would have been out of business this morning. And, of course, the hardest thing to replace would have been his last fifteen years."

"I know," she said. But he knew she didn't. She'd have

146

an instinctive sympathy for Urban, he realized. She was that kind of woman. But she hadn't struggled with the land. She couldn't know what the loss of Urban's place would have meant to him.

"They won't come back, will they?" she asked.

He watched a rider slope unhurriedly down the hill toward them. "If they do, and hit me first, I hope to be ready for them. Or maybe they'll pass me up and land on Tom. . . . Or both of us. Why try to figure it?"

She collapsed the parasol, and put her hands out to him. "Will . . . try to understand us, won't you? Dad doesn't want to be a rebel, but if he makes more fuss than you like, it's only because he's feeling his way. He's never had a ranch resist him the way this one has. Of course, he bought it just at the start of a drought, and it hasn't really broken yet."

"I'll make you a bargain." Will smiled. "I'll try to understand the Cowpers if they'll do the same for me."

She looked up at him earnestly. "I do understand you . . . in most things. But then something happens like last night and I wonder if I understand you any better than I do some Comanche brave."

"Some Comanches," he said, "like their squaws blonde. That's the only resemblance I know of."

The horseman on the road came past a peninsula of cottonwoods, and they saw it was Bill Hamp. Hamp's wide mouth pulled into a stiff line when he saw Starrett. He hauled his horse around, shifting his glance to Lynn. "Your father's looking all over town for you, Miss Lynn."

She smiled. "Isn't he always? Thanks, Bill." She opened the parasol, and laid it back over her shoulder. "Think about it, Will. He can be handled, but not with a spade bit."

She started up the hill. Hamp lingered to roll a cigarette. He said: "One place he can't be handled is where she's concerned."

"He hasn't kicked up much fuss so far," said Starrett.

Hamp glanced at him, making an effort, Starrett thought, to hold the reasonless fury out of his eyes. "If you want peace with him as a neighbor, don't try to make a father-in-law out of him."

Starrett said: "Is this him talking, or you, Bill?"

"It's me that's giving the advice, yes," Hamp snapped. "I'd hate to ram it down your throat, but if you keep him riled up with your moonshining around. . . ."

Starrett hitched his jeans up slowly, his eyes on the ramrod.

Lynn had stopped on the road to call to Hamp, and Hamp stared wordlessly at Will and turned to ride after her.

As he returned to the ranch, Starrett thought: *If there's any danger in him, it's because of her.*

Starrett spread the salt in a wide belt along the foothills. Every morning he studied the sky, but the low, dark cloud did not re-appear. Once he and Cowper met in town and rather sheepishly had a drink. But Bill Hamp drank a little farther down the bar and did not look at Starrett.

Starrett rode home that evening feeling better. Well, you did not live at the standpoint of crisis, and it was not often that something as dramatic as a grasshopper invasion occurred to set neighbors at each other's throats. He felt almost calm and had so thoroughly deceived himself that, when he reached the cut-off and saw the dark smoke of locusts sifting down upon the foothills in the green after-light, he stared a full ten seconds without believing his eyes.

He turned his horse and rode at a lope to his home

place. He shouted at the first 'puncher he saw—"Ride to Urban's for the dozers!"—and sent the other three to the nearest ranches for help. Then he threw some food in a sack and, harnessing a team, drove toward the hills.

There was little they could do that night, other than prepare for the next day. The grasshoppers had landed in a broad and irregular mass like a pear-shaped birthmark on the earth, lapping into the foothills, touching the road, spreading across a curving mile and a half front over the corner of Will Starrett's land.

By morning, eighteen men had gathered, a futile breast-plate to break the grasshoppers' spearhead. Over the undu-lating grassland spread the plague of Mormon crickets. They had already crossed the little area of salt Starrett had spread. If they had eaten it, it had not hurt them. They flowed on, crawling, briefly flying, swarming over trees to devour the leaves in a matter of moments, to break the branches by sheer weight and strip the bark away.

The men tied cords about the bottoms of their jeans, buttoned their shirt collars, and went out to shovel and curse. Fires were started in coulées. The dozers lumbered to them with their brown-bleeding loads of locusts. Wagonloads groaned up to the bank, and 'punchers shov-eled the squirming masses into the gully. Tom Cowper was there with Hamp and a few others.

He said tensely: "We'll lick them, Will." He was gray as weathered board.

But they all knew this was just a prelude to something else. That was as far as their knowledge went. They knew an army could not stop the grasshoppers. Only a compre-hensive thing like fire could do that. . . .

They fought all day and until darkness slowed the grass-hoppers' advance. Night brought them all to their knees.

They slept, stifled by the smoke of grasshoppers sizzling in the coulées. In the morning Starrett kicked the campfire coals, and threw on wood. Then he looked around.

They were still there. Only a high wind that was bringing a scud of rain clouds gave him hope. Rain might stop the grasshoppers until they could be raked and burned. But this rain might hold off for a week, or a wind might tear the clouds to rags. There was rage in him. He wanted to fight them physically, to hurt these filthy invaders raping his land.

When he turned to harness his team, he saw Bill Hamp bending over the coffee pot, dumping in grounds. Hamp set the pot in the flames, and looked up with a taunt in his eyes. Starrett had to discipline his anger to keep it from swerving foolishly against the ramrod.

The wind settled against the earth and the grasshoppers began to move more rapidly. The fighters lost a half mile in two hours. They were becoming panicky now, fearing the locusts would fly again and cover the whole valley.

At noon they gathered briefly. Starrett heard Hamp talking to a 'puncher. He heard the word gang plows before the man turned and mounted his horse. He went over to Hamp. "What do we want with gang plows?"

"We might as well be prepared." Hamp spoke flatly.

"For what?" Cowper frowned.

"In case you decide to fire, Mister Starrett," said Hamp, "and it gets out of hand."

"Shall we put it to a vote?" Starrett asked. An irrational fury was mounting through him, shaking his voice.

"Whenever you say." Hamp drew on his cigarette, enjoying both the smoke and the situation.

Starrett suddenly stepped into him, slugging him in the face. Hamp went down and turned over, reaching for his gun. Starrett knelt quickly with a knee in the middle of his back and wrenched the gun away. He moved back, and, as the foreman came up, he sank a hard blow into his belly. Hamp went down and lay writhing.

"If you've got anything to say, say it plain!" Starrett shouted. "Don't be campaigning against me the way you did Tim Urban! Don't be talking them into quitting before we've started." He was ashamed then, and stared angrily about him at the faces of the other men.

Tim Urban did not meet his eyes. "We've pretty well started, Will," he said. "You've had our patience for thirty-six hours, and it's yours as long as you need it."

Cowper looked puzzled. He stood regarding Hamp with dismay.

After a moment Starrett turned away. "Let's go," he said.

Cowper said: "How long are we going to keep it up? Do you think we're getting anywhere?"

Starrett climbed to the wagon seat. "I'll make up my mind without help, Tom. When I do, I'll let you know."

The sky was lighter than it had been in the morning, the floating contents of cloud leveled to an even gray. It was the last hope Starrett had had, and it was gone. But for the rest of the afternoon he worked and saw to it that everyone else worked. There was something miraculous in blind, head-long labor. It had built railroads and republics, had saved them from ruin, and perhaps it might work a miracle once more.

But by night the grasshoppers had advanced through their lines. The men headed forward to get out of the stinking mass. Driving his wagon, Starrett was the last to go. He drove his squirming load of grasshoppers to the coulée, and dumped it. Then he mounted to the seat of the wagon once more, and sat there with the lines slack in his hands, looking across the hills. He was finished. The plague had advanced to the point from which a sudden strong wind could drive the grasshoppers onto Cowper's land before even fire could stop them.

He turned the wagon and drove to the new campfire blazing in the dusk. As he drove up, he heard an angry voice in staccato harangue. Hamp stood with a blazing juniper branch in his hand, confronting the other men. He had his back to Starrett and did not hear him at first.

"It's your land, but my living is tied to it just as much as yours. This has got to stop somewhere, and right here is as good a place as any! He can't buck all of you."

Starrett swung down. "We're licked," he said. "I'm obliged to all of you for the help. Go home and get ready for your own fights."

Hamp tilted the torch down so that the flames came up greedily toward his hand. "I'm saying it plain this time," he said slowly. "We start firing here . . . not tomorrow, but now!"

"Put that torch down," Starrett said.

"Drop it, Bill!" Tom Cowper commanded.

Hamp thrust the branch closer. "Catch hold, Mister Starrett. Maybe you'd like to toss the first torch."

Starrett said: "I'm saying that none of you is going to set fire to my land. None of you! And you've got just ten seconds to throw that into the fire!"

Bill Hamp watched him, smiled, and walked past the wagons into the uncleared field, into the golden bunch grass. His arm went back, and he flung the torch. In the same movement, he pivoted and was ready for the man who had come out behind him. The flames came up behind Hamp like an explosion. They made a sound like a sigh.

They outlined the foreman's hunched body and poured a liquid spark along the barrel of his gun.

Will Starrett felt a sharp fear as Hamp's gun roared. He heard a loud smack beside him and felt the wheel stir. Then his arm took the recoil of his own gun, and he was blinded for an instant by the gun flash. His vision cleared, and he saw Hamp on his hands and knees. The man slumped after a moment and lay on his back.

Starrett walked back to the fire. The men stood exactly where they had a moment before, bearded, dirty, expressionless. Taking a length of limb wood, he thrust it into the flames and roasted it until it burned strongly. Then he strode back, stopped by Hamp's body, and flung the burning brand out into the deep grass, beyond the area of flame where Hamp's branch had fallen.

He came back. "Load my wagon with the rest of this wood," he said, "and get out. I'll take care of the rest of it. Cowper, another of our customs out here is that employers bury their own dead."

Halfway home, he looked back and saw the flames burst across another ridge. He saw little winking lights in the air that looked like fireflies. The grasshoppers were ending their feast in a pagan fire revel. There would not be enough of them in the morning to damage Lynn Cowper's kitchen garden.

He unsaddled. Physically and spiritually exhausted, he leaned his head against a corral bar and closed his eyes. It had been the only thing left to do, for a man who loved the land as he did. But it was the last sacrifice he could make, and no gun-proud bunch grasser like Hamp could make it look like a punishment and a humiliation.

Standing there, he felt moisture strike his hand, and angrily straightened. Tears! Was he that far gone?

Starting toward the house, he felt the drops on his face. Another drop struck, and another. Then the flood let loose and there was no telling where one drop ended and the other began, as the July storm fell from the sky.

Starrett ran back to the corral. A crazy mixture of emotions was in his head—fear that the rain had come too soon, joy that it came at all. He rode out to catch the others and enlist their aid in raking the grasshoppers into heaps and cremating them with rock oil before they were able to move again.

He had not gone over a mile when the rain changed to hail. He pulled up under a tree to wait it out. He sat, a hurting in his throat. The grasshopper hadn't crawled out of the earth that could stand that kind of pelting. In its way, it was as miraculous as seagulls.

Another rider appeared from the darkness and pulled a winded, skittish horse into the shelter of the elm. It was Tom Cowper.

"Will!" he said. "This . . . this does it, doesn't it?"

"It does," Starrett replied.

Cowper said: "Have you got a dry smoke on you?"

Starrett handed him tobacco and papers.

He smoked broodingly. "Starrett," he said, "I'll be damned if I'll ever understand a man like you. You shot Hamp to keep him from setting fire to your grass . . . no, he's not dead . . . and then you turned right around and did it yourself. Now, what was the difference?"

Starrett smiled. "I could explain it, but it would take about twenty years, and by that time you wouldn't need it. But it's something about burying your own dead, I suppose."

Cowper thought about it. "Maybe you have something," he said. "Well, if I were a preacher, I'd be shouting at the top of my voice now."

"I'm shouting," Starrett admitted, "but I'll bet you can't hear me."

After a while Cowper said: "Why don't you come along with me, when the hail stops? Lynn and her mother will be up. There'll be something to eat, and we can have a talk. That wouldn't be violating one of your customs, would it?"

"It would be downright neighborly," Starrett said.

The Bronc' Stomper

Cal Hawkins was thirty years old, and in a bronc' stomper thirty years is comparable to sixty in a banker. For twelve years he had followed the shows, always paying expenses, sometimes showing a profit. At the end of his last season he showed a net balance of four hundred dollars and seven well-knit fractures. It was getting harder every year to take the jolts. It was becoming more disturbing to shake hands with crippled rodeo bums still riding the circuit for the drinks they could cadge.

After the fall shows, he took a winter job breaking horses. He had made up his mind. He would not go back. He would stay with horse breaking until he had a stake and put it down on a ranch.

The horse-breaking job ended in February, sooner than he had thought it would, but it was like coming out of a cage to be on the move again, drifting leisurely up through New Mexico and waiting for a job to manifest itself. When he heard of a little roping over at Matador, he drifted thirty miles out of his way to watch it. It was an amateur affair, and, being a professional, Hawkins could not compete in it. He merely stood behind the chutes, talking with a couple of cowboys he knew and trying, without being too obvious about it, to get enough of the glorious rodeo smell into his lungs to last a while.

One of the men tried to talk him into making an exhibition ride on a broncho none of the local talent had been able to stay with. "No more outlaws for me," Cal said. "I used to get medical expenses out of riding those brutes, but I'll be danged if I'll ride for less."

But every time a rider came out on a broncho, every time a steer's hoofs thudded down the trampled earth, his hands clenched the chute bars until they ached, the way something inside him ached. He was like a drunkard having his beer, while his throat screamed for the big drink in the little glass. But he stuck to his decision. No more bronchos for Cal Hawkins.

After the show he had a tip that the big Spade Ranch was looking for a horse breaker. Cal tackled Roy Shelly, the manager, in a saloon. Shelly was a lean, old New Mexican with dry, brown skin and a face with more wrinkles than a concertina. He looked like a man who would be contemptuous of anyone who knew less about ranching than he did and hate anyone who knew as much. He had a harassed expression about the eyes and a mouth like a stubborn broncho's.

"Cal Hawkins, eh?" he said. "Do you tame them, Cal, or just put spur marks on them?"

"I give them the three-day treatment," Cal answered. "Ten dollars a head. I'll work steady, if you want. Don't think I'll be riding next season."

"Getting too rich to ride for points?"

"Getting too smart."

Shelly finished his drink. "I'll want a contract, anyway. You don't draw a dollar till you've broke twenty."

They walked down the windy street in the February dusk. "If you're serious about working for a living," Shelly said, "you might do yourself some good out there. Judge Taverner's talking about breaking somebody in as range foreman. Right now I haven't got a man I'd trust to pour whisky out of a boot."

Under a tree in a vacant lot, a wagon was waiting. Shelly hitched the horses while Cal tied his horse and pack animal to the tail of the wagon. Shelly got up on the seat, and filled his pipe. "Joyce ought to be along pretty soon," he said. "The old man's daughter. Not in the contract, by the way. Any taming you do there is out of your own pocket."

A girl hurried from the street with some parcels. She wore a riding skirt and gabardine shirt and a short Chimayo jacket. Her hair, the color of rubbed oak, was long with a clean shimmer. Roy Shelly introduced them. She offered her hand and a smile. She was friendlier than she had to be with a plain horse breaker, Cal thought, and it occurred to him that this job might be less onerous than the average.

As they started out of town, crowded onto the seat, Joyce glanced at him. "I didn't see you ride today, did I?"

"I'm not riding any more," Cal told her.

Joyce smiled. "Well, you'll be able to keep your hand in, in case you ever go back . . . or I don't know the Duke."

Cal was aware of Roy Shelly stirring uncomfortably on the seat. "The Duke?" Cal said.

"Didn't Roy tell you about him? Dad bought him for me last year, but nobody's been able to break him. He's a Morgan-Thoroughbred cross. He'll see that you don't forget how to ride the rough ones!"

Cal glanced at Shelly, but the manager said nothing, and it would have been awkward, just now, to remind him that a horse breaker's job was to break horses, not to make five-gaited saddlers out of them.

When he looked back at the girl, he was not sure he cared to quibble, anyway. Joyce Taverner appeared to be about all a boss' daughter was expected to be—slender, under twenty, and attractive.

★ ★ ★ ★ ★

In the morning, Cal appraised the ranch and liked what he could see of it. The Spade comprised a cattle domain of nearly two hundred thousand acres of unfenced range. The winter grass was yellow, the many dry arroyos were piped with the olive of live oaks, and the hills and mesas were the velvet brown of a riverboat gambler's collar. If you must stay in one place, he thought, it looked like a good place to stay.

Shelly took him into one of the barns to show him a horse in a stall. It was deep slate in color with three white stockings and a blaze on its forehead. It had a wild-eyed stare for them as they moved about.

"One of mine?" Cal asked.

Shelly cleared his throat. "This is the horse Joyce was telling you about. That's a seven-hundred-dollar gelding, son."

Cal liked the massively muscled thighs and forelegs and the small, alert ears. "You mean I ride him for three days, and then she takes over?"

"I . . . uh . . . I thought you could sort of work at it in your spare time."

"In my spare time," Cal said, "I read magazines and play poker. For ten dollars a head I can't make ladies' saddlers out of them."

He said it mainly to let the manager know he wasn't fooled, but Shelly surprised him by saying: "I guess that's right. I tell you what. I'll put up another twenty of my own. I've got a little bet on with the judge about that horse, Cal. He bought him for Joyce on my say-so. Couple of boys have already got pitched off, and now he's crying that the horse'll never be broke. What do you think?"

"I think the song's right . . . 'Never was a man that couldn't be throwed'."

"Think you're the man for this one?"

"Never know till you climb up on them."

They went outside. A screen door banged, and the judge and Joyce came from the house. Judge Taverner was a large, florid, white-haired man who wore a black string tie as a sort of badge of service. His trousers were suspendered high on a capacious stomach, and he had tufted white brows that gave his eyes a penetrating stare.

There seemed to be only one thing on people's minds out here. "What do you think of the Duke, Cal?" Taverner asked.

"Looks all right," Cal said cautiously.

Joyce wanted to know when he was going to start on him.

"Any time," Cal said. "I thought your father would want me to start on the range horses, first."

Taverner glanced at Shelly with those indicative eyes of his. "As a matter of fact," he said, "I'm rather anxious to see what can be done with him. I was persuaded to buy him against my better judgment. I've about decided he's not going to be trained."

Shelly started to reply, but made a hard mouth instead and looked stonily at Cal.

"I'll start him this afternoon, then," Cal said.

In the afternoon, Shelly turned Iron Duke into the corral, and Cal watched him move about. Cowpunchers began to drift over, and the judge and Joyce stood outside the bars with Cal. Iron Duke was pure raw material. He wouldn't lead and he had never worn a bridle. He had a natural single-foot that Cal did not like. He was convinced that horses with natural saddle gaits were apt to be eccentric.

Otherwise, the Duke was a sound and powerful horse, deep-bodied and sensitive. The challenge in his high-held head was his declaration of independence. *So they're trying to make a ladies' horse out of you!* Cal thought. In a way, he and the Duke had something in common. Civilization was trying to make both of them perform tricks they didn't want to.

He advanced carefully with his rope in his hands, talking encouragingly. Immediately the gelding broke and tried to get past him. Cal made his throw so that the horse stepped into the loop. He braced on his heels, and the gray went down.

He went to work quickly, fixing a handkerchief blind and making a hackamore out of the rope. As the Duke lunged up again, he had already begun to sweat. Getting the saddle on him was mayhem, but finally Cal gave the latigo a flip and started the horse toward the gate. One thing he had learned was that it was easier to fall on the ground than on a corral bar.

The Iron Duke was making queer, strangled sounds in his chest. He kicked savagely as Cal turned the stirrup. Cal went up, the gelding tossed off a couple of tentative pitches, and then stood still, trembling. Cal reached forward and yanked off the blinder.

The Duke began to kick and squeal. He started off on a blind run. Suddenly he swerved and began to pitch, putting a neck-breaking snap into it. He tried to shake the saddle loose and bawled like a steer. He ascended in crazy, twisting leaps that turned his belly to the sun.

Up there in the saddle, Cal took the jolting with a frown. It was Iron Duke's privilege to pitch, but he was making a lot of work out of it. He fought as though his honor were at stake.

161

Cal was suddenly ashamed at being involved in it. This horse was no more meant to wear a saddle than Daniel Boone was born to wear white kid gloves. Cal wanted to get it over with. He began to spur. Under the rowelling the gray went wild. He began to pitch toward a tree, and Cal had to slap him on the side of the head with his Stetson to turn him. "Baby," he pleaded, "it's not *that* bad, is it?"

He reached forward to pat the animal on the neck, and at that instant the Duke went into a chain of crow-hops that slammed Cal back and forth from cantle to swell. One of the ranch hands yelled. Cal had lost a stirrup. It flapped wildly, and Cal could be seen stabbing at it with his toe. A moment later he rose out of the saddle, and the Duke went pitching off across the prairie without him. Cal landed on his side and lay there a moment, then got up stiffly.

Joyce ran up. "Are you all right, Cal?"

Cal wiped his forehead with his sleeve. "Yes, but he isn't going to do that saddle any good."

Judge Taverner had a sour grin for him when he and Roy Shelly arrived. "Well, does this prove my point?"

Shelly stared furiously at Cal. Cal didn't know what to say. It was his job to break horses, not to worry about what happened to their souls. He had let Shelly down, because he knew that, although he had not allowed Iron Duke to shake him deliberately, he had gone soft on him for an instant—and accomplished the same thing.

"I wouldn't say that," he told the judge. "He's a scrapper, though. He'll take some doing."

Afterwards, Shelly took Cal aside. "Hawkins, I could've rode out that limber-kneed pitching myself!"

Cal told Shelly: "He puts a mean twist in his pitching. He won't catch me off balance next time."

"If he does, you'll catch yourself hunting a new job."

"I reckon there's one to be had." Cal smiled.

Shelly simmered down. "I'm getting it from both sides, Cal. The judge keeps throwing that seven hundred dollars at me, and Joyce wants her saddle horse. If I had the money, I'd buy the brute myself and shoot him. What do you think . . . is he ever going to make a saddler?"

"If you mean will he ever be any good, I don't know. I've known horses to kill themselves rather than be ridden. We'll find that out when I bring him in again."

He found the saddle five miles out, rolled and kicked to a ruin. But he didn't find the horse, and for a week he kept discovering things to do other than to bring the Duke in. A girl called Rodeo was smiling in his mind again and asking when she would see him. In a few weeks the boys would be throwing their saddles in baggage cars and traveling to wherever the bands played and the prize money was big. But Cal Hawkins would be riding along under hot suns. He would be breaking bronchos and mending fence and flanking calves.

There was only one thing he liked about the job— Joyce—and a small monitor in his mind even shook its head at her. It had started casually, with afternoon rides and long talks. In fact, it was all so relaxed and casual that he let his guard down, and all at once she was dominating even the hours when he was not with her. Right there, Cal halted to look the situation over.

Life with a bronc' stomper would be a non-stop track meet for a girl. Of course, he thought, she might like traveling, but she wouldn't like holing up in two-dollar hotels while her husband tried to win enough money, with his luck running wrong, to bail them out.

Cal was working with a horse one afternoon when she

rode in. It was a crisp March day, the ground still dark with recent rain, a line of sodden clouds on the mesa. She had ridden hard, for her horse was blowing and the impact of the wind had freshened her skin.

"Cal, he's over in Gallina Wash!" she told him. "If we get over there fast, we can catch him."

The horse was at the head of a wide wash peppered with oaks. Just now there was a sandy trickle of water down it. Cal sent Joyce up to start the horse running, and selected a spot behind a shoulder of the cutbank to wait for him.

In a few minutes he heard a yell, and then a soft thunder of hoofs on the sand. Iron Duke flashed past a bend and came out at a reaching lope toward Cal's spot. His mane and tail, a lighter gray than his body, streamed straight back, and his lope was the smooth, co-ordinated run of the wild horse. A tag end of the hackamore still dangled from his neck.

Cal stood there with the rope flung back but without the capability to make the throw. He had broken scores of horses. What was there about this one that upset him?

Suddenly he came alive. He stepped out, swung the rope, and let it stretch across the sand. Iron Duke swerved and ran past.

When Joyce arrived, Cal was simply standing there. She reined up and stared at him. "Cal, you let him get away!"

"*Let* him?" Cal said. "That horse was moving."

"He was moving last time, and you didn't miss. Cal, I think you're afraid of that horse! You don't want to catch him because you're afraid to ride him again!"

Cal looked at her sharply, and swung into the saddle. He started down the wash, but Joyce came up with him.

"Well, isn't that it? You've been finding something to do every day to keep from having to catch him."

"If you want it straight," Cal said, "I *don't* want to break him. There are some horses that weren't meant to be ridden. He's one of them. He may kill himself before he'll be broken."

"But what use is a gelding if he can't be ridden? We can't just let him run wild."

"I'm not thinking about usefulness," Cal told her. It was hard to put it in words because it was merely something he felt. "I'm thinking about his spirit. He's proud. Putting a saddle on him is like putting leg irons on a man. Why humiliate him?"

They rode in silence for a while. Then Joyce said quietly: "The moral seems to be that a horse breaker ought to be like a doctor. He shouldn't get sentimental over his patients. I hope you get over it, Cal, because the Duke is the main reason Roy hired you. Dad thinks you'd fit into this range foreman job he's talking about. But you won't get a chance at it if Shelly fires you."

She was honestly concerned, and it was in his mind to tell her that he wouldn't take such a job because it was the leg irons he had been talking about, but when he thought about it, he knew it wouldn't make sense to anyone but a bronc' stomper.

"I'm no cow rancher," he said. "When I get caught up here, I'll probably move along."

He saw in her face that he had hurt her, and he wished there had been an easier way to break it. She said: "I'm sorry, Cal. I thought you were something more than a bronc' stomper. When you said you'd quit the rodeos, I thought you meant it."

"I thought I did, too," Cal admitted. "Now I'm not so sure. It's hard to break off clean when you've ridden so long. I may ride one more season."

"It's the only way to break off, isn't it?"

"I wish I knew."

They entered the ranch yard. Cal took her horse, but she hesitated a moment. "We don't need to tell anyone we saw Iron Duke. You can go after him later, if you want. I don't want this to spoil your chance at the job, in case you change your mind about staying."

Cal was silent, not knowing what to say—whether to admit that he was afraid to stay because he was falling in love with her, or to find an excuse.

Suddenly her eyes darkened. "You don't have to look so worried, Cal Hawkins! I'm not trying to put a saddle on you. Any girl who took a good look at you would know better!"

She dismounted, threw the reins of her pony over the corral bar, and ran to the house.

Cal sat for an hour on the top pole of a corral, a spot in which he had never failed to find wisdom before, but this time he climbed down with nothing but stiff joints. Yet below the surface of his despair there was an artesian sort of elation that kept bubbling up.

Three more bronchos took Cal's course in how to become cow ponies, and then one day a letter was forwarded from his last address. It was from a promoter who had taken over the little Alpine City rodeo this spring and had the association's blessing on it. Alpine was only fifty miles from the Spade Ranch.

Two thousand dollars in prize money, and championship points will hang on trees. Hope to see you there.

That day he went through the motions of teaching a

horse to lead, but he was experiencing in his mind all the glorious smells and sounds and colors of a big-town rodeo. He got the shakes when he imagined the chute banging open and a broncho cannon-balling through it.

At noon, Roy Shelly tramped into the mess shack. "Take a gander out the window, boys!"

Cal didn't have to look. "Where'd you find him?"

"On the mesa. Had my trap set a week. Well, you got the guts to go up on him again?"

"You want it with a saddle or bareback?" Cal asked.

Shelly said steadily: "You can put glue on your pants if you want, but I want him broke today. Another week of the old man's bellyaching and I'm licked."

Cal went out and looked at the gray. He smoked a cigarette. The horse still wore the hackamore, like a frazzled necktie. But it hadn't put any bow in the proud arch of his neck, for he roamed the corral with those quick, tossing rushes of his that dared a man to come after him.

Someone had told the judge. He and Joyce came out to look him over, and the judge wanted to know what Cal thought about it, would he put up more or less fight after running wild? Cal said probably more, and Taverner went over to harass Roy Shelly.

Cal had been nervous before, but he had never felt like this. He was about to know how a fighter like the Duke looked when he had been utterly subdued, for he meant to stay on his back until he would answer the spur, and the analogy he had drawn between himself and the Duke he could not get out of his mind.

Cal pulled his saddle off the top pole of the corral. This time the Duke anticipated his strategy. It was tougher to throw him and fix the blind. It was a ten-minute campaign to get the saddle on his back. Cal hauled his head around and tried for the stirrup, but the gelding shied off, kicking, until Cal found the stirrup and went up. He threw off the blind and almost instantly the gray's back bent like a spring and he tore loose.

He planted his forelegs, and the horn slammed Cal in the belt buckle. He reached back to bite at his knee. Cal walloped him over the nose with his Stetson and spurred at the same time. Iron Duke blared and shook himself until the saddle popped. Then with his hind hoofs he slashed at the stirrups.

Now he reared, suddenly, pawing at the sky. Cal saw it coming and kicked free. Iron Duke lost his balance and went over backward in a struggling dog fall. The saddle horn cracked against the ground, but Cal had jumped clear and landed on his knees beside the horse.

He was trembling, partly with shock and partly with anger. When the horse scrambled up, Cal was there to seize the reins and vault into the saddle. Iron Duke made a short rush and suddenly realized Cal was still on his back. He went straight up in a sun-fishing leap. As he came back, Cal spurred right and jerked the horse's head left. Off balance, the gray made a futile attempt to crow-hop, and Cal broke that up by reversing the trick. The Duke was baffled. He kept trying to pitch but Cal wouldn't let him. At last he stood shuddering, trying to comprehend it, and Cal went to work on him.

Gradually some meaning began to come out of it. The horse was commencing to understand what the spurring meant. He ran toward the trees. Cal reined in, and he blundered to a stop. Cal spurred, and he made a jerky start. Then Cal and the horse were moving at a long lope toward the mesa.

* * * * *

Cal was back in an hour. Iron Duke was soaked with lather and marked up by the spur. But what the judge and Roy Shelly noticed was that the intangible thing called pride was missing. Iron Duke was just a horse under a saddle—even a little less than that. He was a hangdog creature who had forgotten how to look dangerous. He stood with his legs planted widely as Cal dismounted. He did not respond when Cal patted him and began to loosen the cinch.

Cal started toward the bunkhouse. He paused with his saddle balanced on his hip to say: "Well, boys, I'd say it was a tie match. He's broken, all right . . . plumb broken in two. He'll never be any better than he is right now. But it's not because he was too tough to break. I reckon you were both right."

He walked on, hoping the judge would turn the horse out to range. He had had enough of him. Seeing him now was like coming face to face with himself as he would have been after ten years of punching cows. The Duke had accomplished that much.

In the bunkhouse, he made a roll of his blankets and began dumping his small collection of personal belongings into a sack. In a few days he would be in Alpine City, talking behind the chutes with the boys he had contested against so long, the boys he understood and who understood him. Yet he felt no particular elation over it. He got out the letter and read it again, hoping it would be the trigger to set off the emotions he had expected to feel.

He was standing that way when the light from the door was cut off. Evening sunlight, coming from behind Joyce, made a bright glory of her hair. Her features were in shadow. "Packing?" she said.

"I'm going to make the Alpine City show next week. I may be back. But this one's too good to miss."

Joyce only looked at him.

Cal went on heartily: "Well, he's all yours! You can ride him without a saddle, if you want. Sorry I had to spoil him."

She spoke levelly, as if she wanted to be sure he understood her. "You didn't spoil him, Cal. He spoiled himself. No one could have hurt him if he'd had anything besides pride. You rubbed that off, and there was nothing underneath."

Cal shook his head. "He had as much as any horse ever had. But he hated being bossed a little more than most. That's what ruined him."

Joyce walked up to him. There were tears in her eyes, but what he noticed chiefly was that she seemed angry enough to choke him. "If you don't think you're being bossed by this rodeo thing, Cal Hawkins, you haven't looked at yourself lately. You don't ride because you want to, you ride because you have to. And if you don't have any more spirit and intelligence than a horse, if you're going to keep on being a glorified bum, it's just as well you are leaving!"

The screen door slammed behind her.

Cal thought of a number of things to say, but it was too late, now, and in his bottled resentment he went to stand at the door, frowning after her as she ran into the house. After a moment his displeasure faded. In his mind there remained the impression of her words, and it was like reading clean type after straining too long over a line of blurred print.

He looked beyond the ranch house at the big sweep of prairie suffused with sunset colors. The fluted walls of the mesa were dark, the sky peach and blue. Across the plateau an evening breeze flowed softly. He thought again: *If you must stay in one place, it isn't a bad place to stay.*

He was conscious of the letter, still in his hand, and, as he looked at it, he heard for an instant the distant thunder of hoofs, the yelping of a crowd. But they grew fainter as he listened, dying as inconsequential sounds heard at a distance. Close at hand, the cook began vigorously to hammer the dinner triangle.

Cal jumped. He balled the letter and tossed it in the wood box, and, whistling, he walked toward the washstand to clean up for dinner.

One Man's Gold

I

Casey Brent was dealing faro in One-Ear Jake Digby's gambling hall when Bob Harvey found him. Harvey was known in San Jeronimo as something of a promoter, a man whose interests were diverse, touching cattle, freight, and mining. A considerable piece of his money had gone across the green cloth that evening by the time Casey closed his box at midnight and let another man take over.

Casey Brent had allotted no undue attention to Harvey—no more than any patron received. In his mind, he had him pigeon-holed as a big, easy-grinning man on the corpulent side, baldish, blue of beard, possessed of a bass voice that rattled the chips in the rack. Harvey's jewelry was yellow gold and diamonds, and he lost so pleasantly that it might have seemed the object of the game to lose rather than to win. Thus Casey knew him as a man whose emotions never came to the surface until they had their faces washed and their nails inspected for dirt.

Casey hung his broadcloth coat on a hook at the far end of the bar, and shrugged into a striped gray suit coat. Cut after the fashion, it was tight through the shoulders and chest, not detracting any from his taut, muscled body. Putting on his hat, Casey saw Bob Harvey's florid face in the bar mirror, watching him. As he neared the door, he saw him again, following.

Outside, he put a cigar in his mouth and found a match,

so that, when the cattleman emerged and turned hurriedly to look up the street, a flame flared within two feet of him and Casey's features showed rosily in the glow.

Harvey started, smiled a little sheepishly. "Well, this is right handy!" he said.

"I figured it would be," Casey said. "What's on your mind?"

"Got a few minutes?" Harvey asked.

"I usually grab a little sleep about this time. You weren't figuring on a private game down at the hotel?"

"No," the other man said. "Just a talk with you, Casey. A business proposition. You won't be out much sleep, and you'll stand to make some money easier than running a faro lay-out."

Making the tip of his cigar glow, his glance idling along the dark street beyond the cowman, Casey said casually: "One-Ear's a nice gent to work for. Dealing cards ain't hard work. See you around, Harvey."

"You're a cold customer," Harvey said ruefully. "Tell you what. You give me five minutes, and, if you're not interested in a deal with me, I'll pay you ten bucks for your time and we'll forget it."

"All right," Casey said. "Five minutes."

Harvey poured drinks from a bottle of Scotch in his room, tossed a briefcase onto the bed, and took a chair within reach of it. Casey threw off half his drink, sopped the chewed end of his cigar in the remainder, and returned it to the grip of his strong teeth.

The whisky's warmth was pleasant in his stomach, but it did not reach his narrow, ash-gray eyes. Life had not been kind to Casey Brent. He had rubbed against the rough side of the fabric all his life. He had punched cattle as a kid of fourteen, mucked in mines and worked on a Mexican railroad, and he had dealt cards in every big town from Cheyenne to Monterrey.

Money did not come easily, and he had never learned to hold onto it, mostly because he had never learned how to make a busted flush beat three of a kind. Casey held the conviction that no man was certain of his job but the undertaker, that women were the great mystery, the riddle without solution, and, since he had his teaching about them early and at some expense, he was willing to let the riddle remain unsolved.

He was of sufficient fighting bulk to double as a bouncer on busy nights. He wasn't handsome; his jaw was too wide and square, his chin as aggressive as the tilt of a plug-ugly's derby.

Pensively Harvey ran his fingers about the moist rim of the glass, making the tumbler sing.

"I suppose you know a little about me," he said. "My business is buying up defunct ranches and played-out mines and making them pay. But I'm in a deal right now that ain't looking so rosy. It's what I get for trying to do somebody a favor. Ever been in Socorro, Casey?"

"Been through it."

"Town's a day's ride north of here," Harvey went on. "How I happened to get mixed up in this, I staked a friend of mine to a little iron up there. His name was Ed Lee. I gave him a blank check, told him to find what he liked around ten thousand, and buy it. I agreed to accept ten percent of each year's profits until the note was paid off. The poor damned fool picked out as sorry a spread as you could find. One all-year tank, and he lost that when the government condemned a section of his land for beddin' grounds on the Magdalena trail. Then Ed let all of his cattle get away from him. Finally he saw what looked like an easy out. He wedged the barrel of a Forty-Five-Ninety in the crack of a door, tied a string to the trigger, and blew his brains out. Which left me holdin' the bag."

"You can cry on my shoulder if it will help any," Casey said.

Harvey wasn't smiling now. "I've lost possession of the outfit," he said. "Ed Lee's niece, Katherine Lee, is trying to claim that her uncle left her the ranch."

"Then what you want is a lawyer," Casey said.

"I've got a lawyer." Harvey's big, hair-padded fingers jerked open the briefcase, and he shook out legal-size documents, bunches of cancelled checks and onionskin, letterpress papers. "It's already been through probate, and the court ruled that she has no claim on the Spur Rowel Ranch. But a couple of thick-skulled squatters stole a march on both of us. They're on the land now, hoping the case will drag on until they can market their beef at no cost to them. Names of Ellison and Ashe. I want you to throw those *hombres* off, and then sit down with a gun across your knees and keep Katherine Lee off until I can send some boys to take over. The job's worth three hundred to me."

"You can get gun slicks cheaper than that."

"I don't want gun slicks," Harvey said. "I want a man with enough brains to bounce those men off and keep the Lee girl at bay without raising a ruckus that will mean more delay and expense in court."

Casey frowned, short fingers working at his tough scalp. "I've got a good, steady job right now." He grunted. "Work that I savvy."

"Three-fifty." Harvey sighed.

Casey wagged his head. "That's too good. I reckon the wonder boy is yours. When do I start?"

"Tomorrow morning. Get in touch with Sol Leggett, my lawyer in Socorro. He'll fix you up with an eviction notice on those *hombres*. And good luck, Casey . . . because I'll expect you to earn your money."

II

Armed with Bob Harvey's briefcase, loaded with legal ammunition he might have need of, Casey Brent climbed down from the stagecoach before La Posta Restaurant, stage headquarters of Socorro.

As he stood by the dusty coach with his bag in one hand and the briefcase in the other, he glanced about with the expectation of finding the lawyer, Sol Leggett, there to meet him. But of Leggett there was no sign.

Hostlers took over the blown horses, and Casey looked about. By the restaurant door he saw a pretty, brown-haired girl who had evidently been here to meet the mail. A well-set-up filly, Casey thought. Full-bosom and slim of waist, a young figure and a pert young face. Beyond this, he noticed that her hair was a rich chestnut and that her features had the warm tint of a new ale. That her eyes were a sparkling amber he discovered when he found them watching him.

She approached. Casey's impulse was to retreat. Women and unbroken bronchos—he distrusted both, while being able to appreciate a well-found filly of either class.

She said to Casey: "You're Mister Fountain?"

"If you say so," Casey agreed.

"Oh! I thought you were the man I was expecting on the stage. I'm Katie Lee. Then you aren't . . . ?"

"You keep putting words in my mouth, miss. Sure I'm Fountain."

176

He said it with a bland smile, realizing that perhaps luck had handed him an engraved invitation to insinuate himself into Katherine Lee's confidence.

Katie Lee's smile was a quick flash of relief. "I'm so glad you came," she said quickly. "Your letter didn't make it clear whether you were coming next Saturday or today. I hardly thought you'd have time to make it today." The sun was minting evening gold in the west; the flash of it was in her eyes and hair as she looked up at him. "Suppose we have dinner?" she said. "Then we can talk business."

Casey made serious business of his steak. Katie Lee spoke in such generalities that only a hint of his supposed identity was given him, but that was as Casey had expected. He was a lawyer.

Leaning back, after putting away a slab of apple pie, he lit a cigar. When he met Katie Lee's eyes and saw in them the tense expectancy that ran through her, he knew she was waiting for him to speak.

"Maybe we'd better go over the ground right from the beginning," he suggested.

Katie talked and her story paralleled Harvey's until she spoke of Harvey's motive for backing her uncle.

"Uncle Ed was no rancher, in the first place," she told him. "He was a geology professor until his lungs went bad and the doctor sent him out here. He was the kind who'd sign anything. After four years of trying to make the Spur Rowel pay, he discovered he was paying thirty percent interest to Bob Harvey and hadn't retired any of the principal at all. I was so mad I sent him most of my father's insurance money to pay Harvey off. Uncle Ed did as I asked, and paid me six percent interest and something on the principal last year."

Casey shrugged. "I suppose you know the court will

want proof that Ed Lee paid Harvey before your claim will be recognized?"

"I don't think you read my letter very carefully. I explained that I could find no receipt of any kind after my uncle's death . . . that the only proof I have that he paid Harvey's note is a letter he wrote me."

"Why do you reckon Harvey wants to get the outfit, if it's so sorry?"

"Maybe for the government check for his water hole, waiting for the person who shows title. It didn't come through until after Uncle Ed's death. I've never understood why he sold that spring, anyway. He was hard up enough for water. It was almost as though he had other plans than raising cattle. In fact . . . well, he wrote several times that he was about to strike gold. What he meant by that, I don't know. But Pike Ellison and Poley Ashe must think there is really gold there, because they've been digging ever since Uncle Ed was murdered."

"Murdered! I thought. . . ." His words were cut off.

"That he killed himself?" Katie smiled faintly. "A clumsy attempt was made to make it appear like suicide, but it didn't fool me. But I thought, Mister Fountain, that I explained. . . ."

In his intentness on the conversation, Casey had placed the briefcase on the table and was fooling with the clasps. He saw now that Katie was staring at it, and that into her face had come surprise and fury. The brown eyes, full of sharp light, came up to his, glared right at him, and Katie Lee stood up.

Her face had become red and her eyes filled with tears. Her small hand lashed out suddenly and smashed Casey in the mouth. She hurried out the door and into the dark street.

After she had gone, Casey looked at the briefcase. Small gold letters, punched into the dark brown leather, read as plain as day:

ROBERT L. HARVEY

Casey paid the bill and left, feeling much less clever, almost guilty. But he told himself that, as a man, he was fair prey for every designing female; he had only exercised his just right in tricking Katie Lee into talking. He got a room and, before retiring, sent a telegram to Bob Harvey.

Girl claims Lee paid you off, the telegram said. **Showed letter as proof. How about this?**

There was an answer for him when he came down to breakfast next morning.

Court wouldn't accept her story. Why should you? Not paying you to pal around with her anyway. See Leggett and take care of Ellison and Ashe.

Casey rented a horse at the livery stable and jogged out of town. He reckoned Lawyer Leggett and his eviction notice would keep a day or so more. His instructions how to find the Spur Rowel were plain enough, and he rode from the bosque of the river across an arroyo-slashed tableland that crumpled into oak-clad hills five miles to the east. Here he consulted his landmarks and entered a wide cañon, the floor of which was flat and sandy.

In three miles he saw no cattle or recent sign of cattle. But there was good graze on the slopes of the hills, the better because the yellow bunch grass and gently waving side oats had not been cropped in many months. All that was necessary to make it a paying proposition for a cattleman was water—the treasure over which more men had been killed in the West than gold.

Leaving the main trail, Casey angled along an old cow path to a ridge. Shortly he saw the Spur Rowel buildings below him—one small adobe cabin, two sheds, a neat block of corrals. From this point he proceeded with caution, but despite his searching eyes and the expectant ear he turned to every sound, he was caught with his hand a foot from his gun when he topped a cross ridge and found himself looking down upon a small diggings.

There were several caved-in stopes and a roughly timbered shaft opening from which ran a muddy rivulet of water. There was a faded duck tent. On a rocker in front of a shallow stope a man in a red Cheyenne shirt sat at ease, his gun on Casey.

"There was a nice wide trail a mile back," the scowling-eyed man said. "Why didn't you stay on it?"

"Because I was looking for you," Casey said. "Are you Ashe, or Ellison?"

"I'm Poley Ashe." The cowboy stood up, big and red-faced, black of hair, an over-larded man whose weight had settled in the vicinity of his belt. He wore denims with mud-caked knees and black cowboy boots that had taken a beating from doing a miner's work. In his big hands the .25-20 looked like an air rifle.

"Serve your paper and get ridin'," Ashe said. "Why in hell can't that woman leave us be long enough that we can get some work done?"

"I'm no process server," Casey said. "I'm lookin' for work." The last remark bore the spur marks of hasty thinking.

"Thought you were huntin' me and Pike." Ashe's voice

had a crisp edge of suspicion.

Casey Brent, easing off on the reins and jingling his spurs so that the pony edged forward, made his smile as friendly as though the rifle was not aimed at his face. "That's it. Fellow in Socorro was telling me. . . ."

"Easy with that hoss!"

The pony, head tossing, was edging toward Poley Ashe, and the 'puncher took a backward step. Casey said, pulling the bit sharply into the tender flesh at the back of the pony's mouth: "The cussed skate's been givin' me blazes ever since I left the stable! The critters they'll pass off on a man for a hoss. . . ."

In a sudden stab his spurs went deeply into the soft flanks. The horse jumped at Ashe, squealing, and Casey's hands smacked the swell and he slipped back over the cantle and slid to the ground.

Poley Ashe swore, ducking the horse. There was an instant in which he could have put a rifle bullet into Casey, who was upon him like a cougar. But the 'puncher held his fire, as Casey had figured he would, for with the average man murder is a last resort. The barrel of the .25-20 came into his two big hands and the stock of it swung at Casey's head. In full motion, Casey went to his knees, sliding, sprawling against the cowboy.

Ashe's yell went through the thin mountain air: *"Pike!"*

Casey came up in a rough scramble, throwing his head back as he rose so that it caught the other under the chin. The shock of it staggered both men. But Casey Brent had the heart of a pit bull that fights by impulse until it is utterly whipped. So Poley Ashe felt the slogging pound of fists against his face and body as he stumbled back against the timbered shaft opening.

He was floundering helplessly, his features bruised and

bloody. Beyond him, in the darkness of the tunnel, boo
scuffed and a lamp bobbled into view. With a swing tha
had every muscle of his washboard-sinewed back behind it
Casey knocked Poley Ashe loose of the last of his wrong in
tentions. Ashe made a gasping sound, reached for suppor
that was not there, and fell across an overturned wheel
barrow.

When Pike Ellison came into the yellow glare of sun
light, he stood for a moment blinking down at his partner
He was a baldish, sandy-whiskered man of fifty-odd, lea
and long and tough. He had a .45 in his hand, and h
looked far more capable of using it than had Ashe.

Behind him, Casey said: "Ellison!"

When Ellison turned, Casey hit him in the face with
blow that mashed the man's nose flat and drove him bac
against a stull. Casey tore his gun from him, and tossed i
into the tunnel.

Pike Ellison shook his head, his face flecked with blood
He came at Casey with both hands reaching, and th
shorter, chunkier man struck them aside and chopped vi
ciously at his jaw. Just once. After that Pike Ellison sa
down with his back against the timber and toppled slowl
over on his face. The neck of a pint bottle of whisky stuc
grotesquely out of a back pocket.

Casey had a drink out of the bottle. Presently he loade
the two into the flat-bed wagon standing nearby, trussin
them back to back. He took time to make a cursory exami
nation of the mine lay-out before leaving with his prisoners

The shaft went back only forty or fifty feet. Near th
back the walls oozed water in such quantities that Case
was up to his knees in the run-off. Somewhere he coul
hear a veritable cataract. By lamplight he inspected th
ragged walls of porphyry.

If there was precious metal here, it was in some form Casey Brent did not recognize. Pyrites here and there gave off bright flashes of silver. Other than that he found no ore that even an amateur could have mistaken for gold.

In the tool box he came upon a small bottle with a half inch of sparkling gold flakes in the bottom. Casey poured a quantity in the palm of his hand and bit down on a few flakes. The stuff was gritty. He threw the bottle with its worthless dust upon the ground.

"Pyrites!"

In the middle of the afternoon Casey stopped the wagon short of Socorro and dumped his cursing load of human freight on the ground. He untied the pair.

"Here's as good a place as any to take up your mining operations," he announced. "You'll find as much fool's gold right here as in the hills, and not have to blast to get it. What's more, you'll save yourself and us a lot of future trouble."

"Talkin' about trouble," Poley Ashe's swollen lips muttered, "you've bargained for a heap. Don't get the idea this is finished, mister, because. . . ."

Casey's fist pulled back and the cowboy covered up, backing away awkwardly. Untying the pony from the rear of the flat bed, Casey mounted. "Don't forget to stake out your claim this time, boys," he warned. "The woods is full of sharpers out to ream a couple of honest boys like you."

In Socorro, he bought enough supplies to get by for a week or so at the ranch, until Bob Harvey could come to take over. On the way to the telegraph office, his eye was caught by a shingle swinging in the breeze about the dirt walk: **SOL LEGGETT, ATTY. AT LAW.** Casey's plans underwent swift revision. He turned into the office and found Leggett at a paper-strewn desk. Leggett was a bony rack of a man who looked as though he might at any time dissolve into the same dust that lay thickly over everything in his cell-like office. He acknowledged the gambler's introduction with a corpse-like handshake.

"Began to think Harvey'd given up," he said, indicating a chair. "So you're going to try to pry them boys loose out at the Spur Rowel."

Casey looked at his skinned knuckles. "The fact is," he said, "I've just done it. I thought maybe you could fix it up sorta legal."

"You didn't kill them?" Leggett gasped.

"Well, they squalled like they was killed. But they're rattlin' into town right now in their wagon."

Leggett scowled, arranging and rearranging papers on his desk. "I'll fix it up somehow. Glad there wasn't any gun play. Harvey wouldn't have liked that."

"So he told me," Casey said. "He's dead set against any publicity, ain't he? Almost like he was running a fifth ace into the game somewhere."

Leggett's glance was slow, measuring, full of disapproval. "Did Harvey hire you because you were handy with your fists, or a heavy thinker?" he asked. "Suppose you leave the legal end of this to us?"

Casey shrugged. "Sure. But I was just wondering why he didn't mention to me that Ed Lee was murdered, instead of a suicide."

Slowly the fingers of the lawyer's left hand began to drum on the desk. "Where did you pick that up?"

"From Katie Lee," Casey said. "She also told me that her uncle had paid off that note a year before he was killed. How about that?"

Making no answer, Sol Leggett opened a large checkbook and dipped a steel pen point meticulously into a bottle on his desk. He numbered it, made out Casey Brent as payee, and said without looking up: "You've done a nice job, Brent. How much did Mister Harvey promise you?"

"Oh, I ain't through yet!" Casey exclaimed. "I've just worked up a healthy interest in this. I'm going out and hold down the fort like Harvey asked me to, and maybeso joke around here and there and find out what makes that weed patch so valuable to him and Katie Lee and Ellison and Ashe. First off, I'm going to try and find out how a man could wedge a gun in the crack of a door and pull the trigger with a string. Sort of appears like he'd have to be standing behind the gun to pull that trick."

When he looked back, on reaching the door, he saw those long, pallid hands of Leggett's tearing the check into strips, and he heard him say: "Let me know if you find anything out. I have a feeling that you may."

III

From the appearance of the interior of Ed Lee's cabin, it had not been occupied since the rancher's death. By lamplight, Casey Brent inspected the single, large room that night. He had not yet decided whether Bob Harvey or Katie Lee was the liar. But in the dubious soil Lawyer Sol Leggett's attitude had scattered in his mind, there grew the conviction that Bob Harvey had shown him only the side of the picture that he wanted seen. It went hard with Casey to have to side a woman—any woman—but things were rapidly shaping up that way.

He was intrigued by the manner in which Ed Lee had— or was supposed to have—died. The cabin possessed only one door, and, searching along the jamb, he discovered the spot where the barrel of the rifle had been wedged. He could calculate at about what angle upward the long barrel of the Sharps had pointed. But he could not understand how Lee could have possibly fired it by pulling a string.

The extreme length of the Sharps .45-90 obviated the possibility that he had tied a cord to the trigger, brought it around the edge of the door and back to his hand, for a tug from that position would have brought a forward pull on the trigger instead of backward. There was no ring in the ground beyond the stock of the gun to serve as a pulley, nor could the trigger guard of a Sharps serve as the pulley, for it sloped too obliquely to hold the string in place.

Casey wondered if that had been mentioned at the coroner's inquest. Too, he wondered whether they had looked for the bullet that had killed him. Neither in the cedar *vigas* nor in the willow rip-rapping of the ceiling did he locate a bullet mark. After a half hour's hunt he found a chunk of lead embedded in the last place in the world he would have expected to find it—deep in a corner of the pine drain board of the sink! No upward firing gun could have put it there. The shot must have been fired from about waist height. It was no rifle slug that he dug out. It was an ordinary .45 bullet. In the battered nose he found bits of white that very possibly could have been bone.

Casey was standing with the bit of lead in his hand when something struck with a crash against the cast-iron stove, and ashes and shards of iron flew all over the room. An instant later the sill of a window was splintered, and at the same time Casey heard the sharp report of a rifle.

He blew the lamp out, saw darkness come between him and the men outside like a wall. He was at the back window immediately, thrusting a leg over the sill and dropping to his knees in the darkness. In the black oaks above the cabin a yellow-red ribbon of flame fluttered. Casey did not fire back, not daring to until he knew whether there were other gunmen.

Crawling, he gained the wood shed. In a running crouch he won the manzanita thicket behind the corrals. His boogered pony was kicking up a fuss in the shed, and under the camouflage of this noise he started up the hillside. From the whole set-up he now felt certain he was bucking only one gun.

The killer held his fire among the oaks, playing a waiting game. It was a game Casey savvied, too. He worked toward a shallow arroyo. Reaching it, he made his way to a point somewhat higher than the gunman held. Here he came out again on the slope, to slide silently into a copse of black oak.

Below him, now, he made out the indistinct shape of a man lying behind a log. Casey wormed nearer, holding to a ledge of rock above the motionless figure. The muscles of his legs taut and bunched, he poised momentarily, then sprang. As he did so, he felt his right foot turn in the soft dirt. His poise and his balance were gone. He saw the gunman roll over on his side as he came floundering down beside him.

The ground hit him like a club. Gasping, he hurled himself upon the man and pinned the upswinging gun arm against the ground. His big right fist, deadly as a short arm at close range, flashed down. At the last instant he saw that the jaw he was aiming to break was surprisingly small, clear-lined; the mouth was open, but no sound came out.

Somehow Casey diverted the force of the blow. His knuckles grazed a smooth cheek, and he sat back slowly, staring down at Katie Lee.

After a moment speech came back to her throat. "Will you let go my arm," she said, "so I can get up!"

"Not while you're holdin' onto that Thirty-Thirty," Casey said.

The slim fingers quickly let go of the stock of the Winchester. She lay expectantly, her face, smudged with dirt, very pale against the dark earth. Her body was small and crumpled, and Casey Brent suddenly felt a breathless strength burning in him that was really a weakness, because it was not in him to control it.

He held her, struggling wildly, with his lips against hers. Soon she ceased to fight him, knowing the uselessness of it. Shame came into Brent, then, and he released her. Both of them stood up, and there was an awkward instant in which he waited to be slapped or scratched. Instinct told him that was next in order.

When it didn't come, he muttered: "I'm sorry, Katie. I didn't set out to do that."

Katie rubbed her bruised cheek. "You don't have to apologize. I guess I asked for it when I . . . tried to kill you."

Casey grunted. "You weren't trying to kill me. You could have potted me with that first shot if you'd wanted to. You were trying to scare me out. You can't pull your punches in a game like this and not get yourself in trouble."

"I know," she said wearily. "It's been true of the whole, miserable business. I've been trying to buck a man's game. Well . . . I guess I'm ready to quit."

Casey gripped her arm, suddenly feeling a warm sympathy for her. "No, you aren't, Katie," he said gently. "You aren't the kind to quit until they've run through every card in the deck. How'd you like to have a pardner to back your plays for a while?"

"I don't know what you mean."

"I mean me. I took this job in good faith. Harvey hired me to take possession of the Spur Rowel for him, and I've done it. Now I'm wondering whether it really belongs to him. You told me Ed Lee was murdered. Do you have any proof?"

"Just the fact that he died at a time when his letters were as cheerful as they'd ever been."

Casey showed her the slug he had extracted from the drain board. "This sort of bears you out," he said slowly. "Likely this is the bullet that killed him. I found it in a board inside the cabin. And it wasn't from any buffalo gun. Somebody rigged up that suicide joker after he was murdered."

Katie looked at the bullet, then into Casey's eyes. "Did you mean that about working with me? Because Sol Leggett has got Ellison and Ashe and Harvey all working together against me now. It means odds no smart gambler would risk a nickel on."

Casey retrieved her rifle, and handed it to her. "Let's go down and have a cup of java before you go back . . . pardner."

In the wreckage of the cook stove, Casey re-heated his supper coffee and poured two cups. As they drank, he tried to rally his ingrained suspicions of women as a whole, but for Katie he could find nothing but warmth. She had courage, and she was pretty. He was unconscious of staring until she rose, coloring, and moved toward the window.

"I didn't do the place any good," she remarked. "Look at that stove. And this window . . . *Casey!*"

The tone she used was a command that brought him to her side. He looked down with her at the window sill, shattered by her second shot. A piece of board had been blasted away so that a hollow space was revealed beneath. Casey could see what looked like papers inside. He used the barrel of his .45 to pry the rest of the board loose. Then he took out a bunch of papers and cancelled checks, fastened together by a string.

Katie went through them, her face full of color, her eyes shining. She was not long in separating a single check from the rest. She exhibited it to Casey in triumph.

"Uncle Ed's cancelled check!" she cried. "As good as a receipt!"

On the back of the draft Ed Lee had printed: **The undersigned, in endorsing this check, accepts it as final payment on note held by him against E. R. Lee**. And Bob Harvey's bold, aggressive hand had inscribed his name below.

"That puts the skids under Harvey." Casey grinned. "Stick that thing in a safety deposit vault tomorrow morning. We'll have the Spur Rowel in your name before he knows what's happened."

"Why would he try to run a bluff like this," Katie wondered, "knowing the receipt might be found at any time? Do you suppose he believes the story about Uncle Ed's finding gold?"

"Plenty of people seem to," Brent said quickly. "But all I found up there was mud and rocks. There'll be time to size up this outfit after we get things under control. We'll talk to a lawyer tomorrow morning. Then I'm going to set a charge of dynamite in that mine that'll decide once and for all whether there's any gold in the hill."

He met Katie at the hotel in the morning. They had breakfast and were on the point of leaving when several men, talking loudly, entered the room. They took a table near the front. A voice catching at Casey's memory, he turned—and met Bob Harvey's glance across the room.

Harvey was with Poley Ashe, Pike Ellison, and Sol Leggett. Leggett had not yet sat down. He was hanging his hat on a hook near the door, but, as Casey Brent left his table, Leggett put his hat on quickly and backed out the door.

Casey looked down into Harvey's florid face, noting that he had not shaved in some time and that road dust emphasized every crease of his dark coat. In his eyes there was a pinch of fatigue. He had come in a hurry, it was Casey's guess, in response to Leggett's hasty summons. Just how he and the erstwhile squatters had come to pool their interests left room for conjecture.

Presently Harvey snapped: "Sit down."

Casey shook his head. "No," he said. "Suppose you get on your feet."

Harvey studied him, and Ellison and Ashe, their faces battered, were wary. "What's the idea?" Harvey asked, at length. "I pay you to do a simple job, and you get the idea you're Wild Bill Hickok and Sherlock Holmes combined. I'm going to pay you the three-fifty, Brent, and then I want to see you ride out of here and find somebody else's business to poke your nose into."

"I thought this was all on the up-and-up," Brent said gently. "Is there something you don't want me to catch on to?"

Harvey pulled a billfold from his coat, and counted a small pile of bills onto the tablecloth. "There's your money. Take it and get out."

"I hope you haven't got yourself all messed up in this deal over that gold mine of Ed Lee's. Because it's my hunch there ain't as much gold up there as you've got in your hind teeth. If you murdered the old gent for that, the devil's probably laughing himself sick in hell, right now."

Bob Harvey stood up, quick and easy in his movement for all his bulk. The two 'punchers stood up, too, ready to follow where he led. "Did you say . . . murdered?" he asked.

"I said murdered . . . bushwhacked. I can prove Ed Lee didn't die by his own hand. I can't lay the job at anybody's doorstep just yet, but I've still got some hunches to work on. And, by the way, I found the check Lee gave you when he paid off the note. It begins to look like you played me for a sucker. Just like you're playing these two bronc'-brained culls right now . . . working both ends against the middle. It makes me sore enough to hang one right on your jaw. In fact, I think. . . ."

But Harvey anticipated the move, and his own fist came up and caught Casey in the stomach. The gambler grunted. Harvey spilled the table against him, and came on. The sick pain of that blow to the groin was all through Casey, slowing him, weighting his arms. He stabbed at Harvey's face. Harvey's fist cocked—and held.

A man said: "Now, now, gents. This is a hotel, not a saloon. Besides, it ain't necessary. I got a warrant here for your arrest, Brent. Assault with intention to commit murder is the charge. Ellison and Ashe, the plaintiffs."

Casey looked into Marshal Charlie Grimes's sunburned face while the officer took his gun. Sol Leggett was back in the doorway, almost smiling for once.

"This is what happens to tinhorns that don't stay on their own range," he explained. "What made you think you could horn in here, Brent? The game was already crowded."

Casey saw Katie Lee coming forward, and he shook his head slightly, his eyes sharp with warning. "What's the bail set at, Marshal?" he asked.

"No bail," Grimes said. "This is a hangin' charge, if the

judge is minded to throw the book at you."

Harvey chuckled, and Casey's head turned angrily. "I'll bust this charge!" he told him. "And when I get out, I'm coming after you. I'll take out my pay in hide . . . a nickel a square foot. All you're going to mine on the Spur Rowel is trouble and plenty of it."

Charlie Grimes, who had listened to badmen's promises before, winked at Harvey. Casey Brent saw the momentary relaxing of vigilance and acted. He pivoted and sank his fist deeply into Grimes's belly. He tore his own captured Colt from the marshal's hands and the lawman's as well. Immediately he had all five men under his sights and was backing toward the door. Grimes was down on the floor, groaning.

"Sorry, Marshal," Casey said. "You and me and these here plaintiffs are all in the same boat . . . buckin' one another for the benefit of Bob Harvey. I'll buy you a drink for the loan of your gun, someday, when I come back to pay Harvey what I owe him."

Gaining the dirt walk, he was out of their sight in one stride. At the hitch rack, he lingered to drive a shot through the doorway, and the explosion rang harshly along the quiet morning street. Casey heard the jangle of broken crockery, and he hit the saddle, and went like a cannon ball up the street, riding close to the row of chinaberries on the west side of the road.

Before he made the turn, he saw bark fly from the trunk of a tree just ahead, heard the *pop* of other bullets striking adobe house fronts and chinaberries close to him. He put the corner of a building between himself and the gunfire. Before him lay a narrow way that broke back into a scattering of small *jacales* and finally became a dusty wagon road disappearing into the bosque of the river.

Casey rode through the brush and into the river. He

went at a hard, pounding lope downstream a few hundred yards. Then he came out on the west bank. With the mesquite and willow tangles for a screen, he proceeded more slowly farther down, hearing behind him the sounds of men and horses trying to pick up his trail. But Casey's pulse was even and his mind at ease. He'd played this game against experts, and Bob Harvey was no expert.

Leaving the bosque miles south, he rode slowly, trying to decide where the swift race of events of the last couple of hours had brought him. For whipping Poley Ashe and Pike Ellison, a jury might give him a few months, probably no more than that. But it would leave him unable to help Katie Lee. Strangely that was the thing that kept his heavy brow plowed with worried lines. Up to last night, he had considered women, one and all, as a class—like lawyers and tinhorn gamblers. Paradoxically his attitude toward Katie had altered when she had let a couple of Winchester slugs loose in his direction. She was making a game fight, and Casey liked a fighter.

About noon he came warily out upon a knoll above the Spur Rowel buildings. He searched for signs of a trap, found nothing to arouse suspicion, and rode into the oaks, where he left his pony while he approached the cabin. Casey listened outside the back window. He poked his head inside, then, and made sure that the place was empty.

In the window sill strongbox he retrieved the rest of the papers they had found, all but the cancelled check. He went through them thoroughly, sorting, studying. He wanted most of all to figure out what kind of a man this Ed Lee had been, for if he could learn that, he might save himself a lot of trouble. Had he been a hard, steady worker, or a harebrained glory holer? Was he intending to make the Spur Rowel a paying proposition someday, or had he pinned a lot of tinseled hopes on that coyote hole up in the hills?

Casey thumbed through a thin sheaf of government bulletins on cattle raising. He pored over a score of government contour maps of southwestern New Mexico. He inspected geological reports of the section. Ed Lee seemed to have been a man of varied interests.

A book of check stubs furnished him with something to work on. Expenditures were listed for cases of dynamite, for a star drill, for a wheelbarrow, but no rocker, no flasks of mercury, no acids—none of the equipment of the gold miner.

It was just as he was beginning to make some sense out of these disconnected clues that he heard iron shoes ring cleanly on the trail. Casey was out of the chair instantly and pressing beside a front window. He had his cheek against the smooth walnut of his rifle stock, and he watched a paint pony come into the notch of his sights. When he saw Katie's hair burn golden in the sunlight, he grunted, lowered the gun, and stepped to the door.

He met her at the corral and helped her down, and for a moment that same breathless urge that had held him last night came into him as her soft hair brushed his face. But he set her down, holding her hands as she looked up at him.

"This will teach you never to trust a woman again, Casey," she said, and she was only half bantering. "You were doing all right until you tried to help me out, weren't you? I'm sorry you had to get mixed up in it. But if I'm ever able, I'll pay you back for all you've done."

Casey was suddenly embarrassed. "Forget it," he told her. "Dodgin' law's a nice change from dealing faro, anyway. What happened after I left?"

"Harvey put up a thousand dollars reward for you. He's afraid of you, Casey. He thinks you've really found out something about how Uncle Ed died."

"I wish I had," Brent said slowly. "As it is, I've got the law dogs barkin' at my heels instead of his. Did you put that cancelled check in a safe place, like I told you?"

He could see that his words gave her a start. "I forgot," she admitted. "I put it in my desk at the hotel, and it's still there."

"We hope," Casey said. "Well, you can help me out a little before you go back. I've been studying this gold mine proposition. Frankly I don't think you're going to find anything in that hole. But your uncle was a geologist, and he must have had some reason for sinking it. I'm going to find out what it was." Katie's eyes questioned him, and Casey went on. "There's about a dozen sticks of dynamite up there. I'm going to drill a hole as long as his drill will cut and fill it up. I may bring the whole hill down, but at least we'll know what Ed Lee was looking for."

"How can I help?"

"You're going to hold the drill for me and take a gander around, now and then, so that they won't sneak up on us. I haven't swung a single-jack in so long that I may take your head off with the first swing, though. Are you game to take a chance?"

Katie lifted her foot to the stirrup. "Get your horse," she said.

IV

There was one lamp cap in the toolbox. This Casey lighted and gave to Katie. He trimmed a coal-oil lantern, and with its cheerful glow swinging along before them they started into the mine. The water was deeper than ever. Casey thought about a cave-in, but a glance upward showed only ragged facings of tuff and porphyry, hard as iron. Up and down the shaft played will-o'-the-wisp lights, glancing off the icy surface of the water from their lamps.

Here and there Casey stopped to inspect a fault. Near the back he discovered a crack from which a bucket or two of water per minute was pouring down the wall. An idea began to take shape in his mind.

He made a painstaking inspection of the rock structure at dead end. Selecting a spot for the charge, he showed Katie how to hold the star drill, giving it a quarter turn after each blow of the sledge. Casey had put the full power of his shoulders into many a stroke of the single-jack, but he had never felt the raw tingling of his nerves as he did now. He stood with the hammer poised over his shoulder, up to his knees in the water, noticing how close to the girl's head the sledge must pass to deliver a full-bodied blow.

Katie knew what he was thinking, and without looking up from her job she said: "Going soft, Casey? I thought you could swing one of those things."

A spark glinted on the head of the single-jack. Casey hit the drill fully and cleanly and heavily. Katie didn't flinch. Her hands gave the steel bar a quarter turn, but Casey could see the tight set of her lips.

For ten minutes they worked without pause, without rest for either. Then Casey dropped the sledge. He took off his shirt, wet with perspiration.

"Take a look around outside," he said. "If you see anything you don't like, give me a holler."

Before long she came wading back. "Nothing in sight. How much longer will this take?"

"Maybe an hour. On the job, kid."

With intervals of rest, they continued to drive the drill deeper into the porphyry. Katie Lee was almost finished.

Her hands had lost the snap with which she had handled the drill. At length Casey lowered the sledge-hammer for the last time.

"That'll do 'er. Let's get some air."

The sunlight was a hot blast against Casey's bare flesh. He stood before the tunnel a moment, his glance ranging along the ridge that loomed above the mine. In the warm stillness of the late afternoon there was no sound but the whisper of a breeze through the manzanita thickets.

Casey put a coil of fuse over his shoulder and picked up the box of dynamite. "I'll finish up," he said. "Keep your eyes peeled and be ready to run when I come back. This is liable to blow the top off the damn' hill."

He shoved into the hole all the dynamite it would take. Onto his fuse he fixed a cap, biting down hard with his teeth. Putting the cap in place, he strung out a good length of fuse, lacing it along a rough ledge two feet above the water level.

At the last instant he touched a match to the ready powder core. With the angry hiss and sputter in his ears, he began to wade clumsily back toward that point of light fifty feet away. He was halfway to the opening when he heard Katie Lee scream.

Casey stopped. He could hear, indistinctly, the sounds of a struggle. That stopped his momentary notion of returning to put out the fuse so that he could make a stand here without being blown to hell. Katie was in trouble. That made a big difference with Casey.

He left the tunnel on the dead run. Again the impact of sunlight against his eyes was a dull, hurting force. He made out a struggling shape off to the left, and sprang that way. But something heavy and blunt came down on the side of his head, and he was down in the dirt, his senses spinning.

When he came up, Harvey was standing beside him and Katie sat on a rock between Poley Ashe and Pike Ellison. "So this is why you pulled the double-cross on me," Bob Harvey said. "One more ambitious *hombre* trying to horn in here. I thought you said there was no gold in this mine."

"Did somebody say there was?"

Harvey's red, blunt features were impatient. "You aim to run your bluff right down to the shank, do you? Ain't you convinced yet that you hold a busted flush?"

Casey said, his lips tightly drawn: "I'm convinced that we're all going to get blown right out of the picture if we stay here about thirty seconds longer. I just set a charge in there!"

Harvey laughed. "I give you credit for working all the angles. No, Casey, it's showdown this time. And the first thing I want is a cancelled check with my name on the back. One of you two's got it, because it wasn't down at the cabin. You can save yourself . . . and the girl . . . a lot of unpleasantness by handing it over."

Casey stood up, his legs unsteady, his heart slogging wildly. "I'm not bluffing this time! There's five sticks of powder. . . ."

Harvey snorted: "Oh, hell! Stand the girl up, Poley."

Poley made Katie stand up, and Harvey waited a moment, and then struck her savagely across the face with the back of his hand. Pike Ellison knew his job for he kept Casey under his sights and his eyes were mean, full of venom.

Poley held the girl while Bob Harvey hit her a second time. "This is only practice," said the cattleman. "But I can be downright cruel if I have to. Why don't you show me that you've got more sense than your uncle had by coming across? I offered to buy him out, but he hung on for a better price until we had to reach a settlement of a different kind. I want that check . . . now."

"I . . . I haven't got it." Katie's eyes were wide, her face so pale that her eyes were dark blotches.

Casey Brent's voice went through the pause, low and unhurried. "I'm comin' at you, Harvey. I'm saying you haven't the guts to face me in a man's fight, even with your pardners to back you up with guns if I fist whip you."

Bob Harvey swung to face him, said with a hard bite: "Then keep coming. You've blowed off about how tough you are until somebody's got to show you." He stripped off his coat as Casey stopped there, just short of the mine entrance.

"Give 'im double-barreled hell, Bob!" Pike Ellison said, watching Harvey to go meet the stocky, broad-shouldered gambler who waited with his fists on his hips.

Just before Harvey reached him, Casey tagged him with a jab in the belly, stopping the cattleman squarely in the entrance to the tunnel. Harvey swore and waded in, but again Casey reached through his guard to find his jaw. This time the heavier man stumbled back against the stull.

Instead of following up his advantage, Casey Brent took a step back. Bob Harvey wiped the back of his hand across his mouth. He came away from the tunnel, more slowly this time, and he was standing precisely in the center of the drift when the dynamite exploded.

Casey saw a blast of air pick up the cattleman and carry him like a leaf in a gale. The air was filled with chunks of rock and with a mixture of mud and splintered timbers. One of the rocks caught Harvey in the back and pinned him against the rocker. It was a grisly sight Casey would not forget.

Even while he was watching Harvey, he himself was

stumbling about like a drunken man. The ground was like jelly, shifting fantastically under his feet. Casey's head was filled with the roar and ring of the angry gases. He saw the mine entrance come down with a crash, and then the thing he had been waiting for happened. A great, muddy, leaping head of water belched from the hillside. Harvey's body was picked up by the torrent and carried down the slope to an arroyo. Pike and Poley watched, paralyzed. Before either man moved, Casey was upon Poley Ashe.

Poley carried a carbine, and it was upon the .30-30 that Casey's hands closed. He tore the carbine from the man, and stepped back to cover him and his partner.

Pike was dropping behind a rock at the edge of the water. Casey slapped the carbine to his shoulder as Ellison threw down. The slug caught the man in the center of the chest, knocking him back into the water. The stream tugged at him as he lay on his back, pulling him slowly, without resistance, after Bob Harvey.

It was a blue chip game that Poley Ashe could not leave after having anted so much. Casey Brent's shouted warning did not stop him. He went after his Colt, and had raised it almost to firing position before the other man shot. Ashe sank down, his gun blasting into the dirt before him. He tried to fire once more, but it was reflex action, for Casey's lead had gone through his heart.

At sundown, on the trail back to Socorro, Casey Brent and Katie came upon a small, muddy stream in Dry Cañon, where they had forded no water on the way in. It was a brave little creek hardly more than a trickle, but Casey murmured: "There's Ed Lee's gold. There'll be a dozen all-year tanks on this iron, now. Wish the old-timer could have lived to see it."

Katie's eyes said that this muddy ribbon of water did not look like gold to her, and Casey explained.

"Your uncle was geologist enough to know that there wasn't likely any gold up here. He knew the only way he'd ever make anything out of the Spur Rowel was to get water. So he got himself a flock of contour maps and studied the lay of the land and the conformation of the hills until he knew just about where a man would have a chance of hitting water. Probably there was a spring up yonder, and he started digging to turn it into a tank. That was when he found out there was a real stream underground. I could tell by the way he'd angled his drift into the hill, not trying to follow the ledges and faults, that it was no ordinary mine."

"And Bob Harvey saw his diggings and thought he was after gold," Katie said.

"Harvey killed him for it, and cashed in his own chips trying to grab a little two-bit iron he could have duplicated any day in the week."

They crossed the stream, riding for a while in silence. "A two-bit iron is what it is," Katie admitted, "and I'm ashamed to ask any self-respecting man to manage it for me. But I'd like to wish the job on you, Casey."

"I might take it," Casey said, "on the basis of a long-term contract. Say about forty years."

Katie Lee showed that she was a properly brought up girl by not smiling, even when he took her hand. "We'll take that up later," she said. "After we know each other better."

"Sure. I'll ask you again in about five minutes. The rate we've been getting acquainted, we'll be old friends by then."

Again they rode in silence. Casey was thinking that every man prized his own kind of gold. To Ed Lee it had

meant water; to Bob Harvey it had been money. For Casey.
. . He was watching the sun pick up red-gold threads from
Katie's hair, and he reckoned his kind of gold was the most
precious of all.

About the Author

Frank Bonham in a career that spanned five decade achieved excellence as a noted author of young adult fi tion, detective and mystery fiction, as well as making signi icant contributions to Western fiction. By 1941 his fictio was already headlining Street & Smith's *Western Story* ar by the end of the decade his Western novels were being se alized in *The Saturday Evening Post*. His first Wester LOST STAGE VALLEY (1948), was purchased as t basis for the motion picture, STAGE TO TUCSON (C lumbia, 1951) with Rod Cameron as Grif Holbrook ar Sally Eilers as Annie Benson. "I have tried to avoid Bonham once confessed, "the conventional cowboy stor but I think it was probably a mistake. That is like trying avoid crime in writing a mystery book. I just happened to more interested in stagecoaching, mining, railroading. . . Yet, notwithstanding, it is precisely the interesting—and comparison with the majority of Western novels—exot backgrounds of Bonham's novels that give them an adde dimension. He was highly knowledgeable in the technic aspects of transportation and communication in the 19t Century American West. In introducing these backgroun into his narratives, especially when combined with his fir grasp of idiomatic Spanish spoken by many of his Mexic characters, his stories and novels are elevated to a high plane in which the historical sense of the period is alwa very much in the forefront. This historical aspect of h Western fiction early drew accolades from reviewers so th on one occasion the *Long Beach Press Telegram* predicted that "when the time comes to find an author who can best fill the gap in Western fiction left by Ernest Haycox, it may be that Frank Bonham will serve well." Among his best Western novels SNAKETRACK, NIGHT RAID, THE FEUD AT SPANISH FORD, and LAST STAGE WEST.

About the Editor

Bill Pronzini was born in Petaluma, California. His earliest Western fiction was published under his own name and a variety of pseudonyms in *Zane Grey Western Magazine*. Among his most notable Western novels are STARVATION CAMP (1984) and FIREWIND (1989). He is also the editor of numerous Western story collections, including UNDER THE BURNING SUN: WESTERN STORIES (Five Star Westerns, 1997) by H.A. DeRosso, RENEGADE RIVER: WESTERN STORIES (Five Star Westerns, 1998) by Giff Cheshire, and TRACKS IN THE SAND by H.A. DeRosso (2001).

Additional Copyright Information

"City of Devils" first appeared in *New Western* (4/48). Copyright © 1948 by Popular Publications, Inc. Copyright © renewed 1976 by Frank Bonham. Copyright © 2003 by Gloria Bonham for restored material.

"The Last Mustang" first appeared in *Blue Book* (8/49). Copyright © 1949 by McCall Corporation, Inc. Copyright © renewed 1977 by Frank Bonham. Copyright © 2003 by Gloria Bonham for restored material.

"River Man" first appeared in *Argosy* (12/31/41). Copyright © 1941 by The Frank A. Munsey Company. Copyright © renewed 1969 by Frank Bonham. Copyright © 2003 by Gloria Bonham for restored material.

"Payment Past Due" first appeared in *Dime Western* (7/48). Copyright © 1948 by Popular Publications, Inc. Copyright © renewed 1976 by Frank Bonham. Copyright © 2003 by Gloria Bonham for restored material.

"Good Loggers Are Dead Loggers" first appeared in *Dime Western* (11/48). Copyright © 1948 by Popular Publications, Inc. Copyright © renewed 1976 by Frank Bonham. Copyright © 2003 by Gloria Bonham for restored material.

"Burn Him Out!" first appeared in *Argosy* (9/49). Copyright © 1949 by Popular Publications, Inc. Copyright © renewed 1977 by Frank Bonham. Copyright © 2003 by Gloria Bonham for restored material.

"The Bronc' Stomper" first appeared in *Blue Book* (7/49). Copyright © 1949 by McCall Corporation, Inc. Copyright © renewed 1977 by Frank Bonham. Copyright © 2003 by Gloria Bonham for restored material.

"One Man's Gold" first appeared under the title "Satan Hires a Gambler" in *10 Story Western* (8/42). Copyright ©

1942 by Popular Publications, Inc. Copyright © renewed 1970 by Frank Bonham. Copyright © 2003 by Gloria Bonham for restored material.

Foreword copyright © 2003 by Bill Pronzini.

GUNS OF VENGEANCE

LEWIS B. PATTEN

Incessant heat and drought have taken their toll on the Wild Horse Valley range. And nowhere is it worse than on the Double R, the largest ranch in the district, owned by Walt Rand. Things really heat up when Nick Kenyon diverts what little water is left in Wild Horse Creek, giving his little ranch more water than it needs and the Double R none. Kenyon had long since managed to turn all the smaller ranchers against the Double R, blaming Rand and his greed for all the problems on the range. But stealing water in a drought is the last straw, and Rand decides to fight back. He'll deal with Kenyon the same way he would with anyone who stole what belonged to the Double R—with bullets!

Dorchester Publishing Co., Inc.
P.O. Box 6640   ___5376-4
Wayne, PA 19087-8640 $4.99 US/$6.99 CAN

Please add $2.50 for shipping and handling for the first book and $.75 for each additional book. NY and PA residents, add appropriate sales tax. No cash, stamps, or CODs. Canadian orders require an extra $2.00 for shipping and handling and must be paid in U.S. dollars. Prices and availability subject to change. **Payment must accompany all orders.**

Name: _____

Address: _____

City: _____ State: _____ Zip:_____

E-mail: _____

I have enclosed $_____ in payment for the checked book(s).

CHECK OUT OUR WEBSITE! www.dorchesterpub.com.
_____ Please send me a free catalog.

ATTENTION BOOK LOVERS!

CAN'T GET ENOUGH
OF YOUR FAVORITE WESTERNS?

CALL 1-800-481-9191 TO:

- ORDER BOOKS,
- RECEIVE A FREE CATALOG,
- JOIN OUR BOOK CLUBS TO SAVE 30%!

OPEN MON.-FRI. 10 AM-9 PM EST

VISIT
WWW.DORCHESTERPUB.COM
FOR SPECIAL OFFERS AND INSIDE
INFORMATION ON THE AUTHORS
YOU LOVE.

LEISURE BOOKS
We accept Visa, MasterCard or Discover®.